# Claudia Talks Family

I love playing the violin. Or at least I used to. That was when I thought the violin was important to my family. Before I found out that it didn't matter to them at all.

My name is Claudia Salinger. You've probably heard about my family. Everyone at school knows the story. We live alone in my house—just my brothers, my sister, and I.

My parents died in a car accident two years ago, when I was ten. That's when my oldest brother, Charlie, became our legal guardian. He's twenty-five, so I guess everyone figured he was old enough to take care of us. But sometimes he really messes things up. Like the time he forgot to pay the electric bill. We lived in the dark for a week!

But it's okay when Charlie makes a mistake. Bailey is always there to fix it. He's my other big brother. He's in college, and he's the coolest. Whenever I have a problem, I ask Bailey for help. Like when I'm afraid I might forget how my parents' voices sounded. Or how they looked. Bailey says my brothers and sister will always be there to help me remember.

My sister, Julia, reminds me of my mother sometimes. She's really smart and pretty, like Mom was. Julia is in high school. I want to be just like her when I'm seventeen!

Then there's Owen. He's only two. But I can tell that someday he's going to be a brain surgeon or something. He already knows how to spell my name with his blocks. He's *so* smart. I think he takes after me!

My brothers and sister are always busy with school or work or girlfriends and boyfriends. And I'm always busy practicing my violin. The violin reminds me of my mom. Charlie says I inherited her talent. Mom used to play with one of the best orchestras in the country. Maybe one day, I'll do the same thing.

Sometimes we get so busy that we don't see one another enough. That's why we eat dinner together every Friday. We go to Salinger's, the restaurant my dad used to own. They always have our table reserved—for a party of five.

*Claudia*

**PARTY OF FIVE™: Claudia**

Welcome to My World
Too Cool for School

Available from MINSTREL Books

# party of five™

# Claudia

## Welcome to My World

Elizabeth Winfrey

**Based on the television series
created by Christopher Keyser
& Amy Lippman.**

A
MINSTREL®
BOOK

Published by POCKET BOOKS
New York   London   Toronto   Sydney   Tokyo   Singapore

A MINSTREL PAPERBACK *Original*

A Minstrel Book published by
POCKET BOOKS, a division of Simon & Schuster Inc.
1230 Avenue of the Americas, New York, NY 10020

A PARACHUTE PRESS BOOK

ISBN: 0-671-00676-2

First Minstrel Books printing March 1997

10  9  8  7  6  5  4  3  2  1

Printed in the U.S.A.

# Welcome to My World

# chapter one

*Ladies and gentlemen, Claudia Salinger." The announcer's voice boomed through Carnegie Hall. As I walked out onto the stage, the crowd rose in a standing ovation. I smiled, then lifted my violin to my shoulder.*

*"Thank you for coming," I said into the microphone. I placed the bow of my violin against the strings. I began the first notes of Mozart's* Violin Sonata in G. *Just then, a loud, shrill scream echoed from the balcony. My first concert was ruined!*

I squeezed my eyes shut, willing myself to go back to sleep. But the beeping of the alarm clock next to my sleeping bag was getting louder by the second. I opened one eye and peered at the digital clock: seven A.M.

I punched the snooze button and closed my eyes again. Just another fifteen minutes. Maybe I could even get back my dream. *You're in Carnegie Hall, and the crowd loves you,* I told myself.

Forget it! My eyes popped open again. I wasn't at Carnegie Hall—I was at home in San Francisco. A warm tongue was licking my face.

"Thurber, how did you get in here?" I asked as I sat up.

Thurber, our bulldog, gazed at me with his big brown eyes and wagged his stubby tail. I leaned forward and examined the flap of my tent. Yup—it was open. I guess I forgot to zip it up all the way when I went to sleep last night.

I know most twelve-year-old girls have their own bedrooms, with pink comforters and flowered curtains. But I'm not like most twelve-year-old girls. I sleep in a blue and gray camping tent set up right in our dining room. And all my clothes are in the hall closet.

I used to share a room with my seventeen-year-old sister, Julia. That was before our parents died in a car crash two years ago. After the accident Julia moved into their room.

My oldest brother, Charlie, wasn't hanging around the house much in those days. He had his own apartment. When Mom and Dad died, Charlie became our legal guardian. He didn't mind sleeping on the couch whenever he spent the night at our house. But then he realized he had to live here full-time if our family was going to stay together.

Charlie kicked Julia out of the master bedroom and took it for himself. Julia was in her "I'm a moody teenager who needs complete privacy" phase. She absolutely refused to share a room with me.

The tent was my idea. It's all mine—and I get to overhear a lot of private conversations, since people don't always realize when I'm in my tent.

"Move, Thurber," I commanded. He didn't move. "Come on, let's go." He just kept staring at me. "Biscuit!" I told him.

Thurber ran right out of the tent—the thought of food is the only thing that ever gets him moving.

I followed him out into the dining room. The house was quiet. My brothers and sister were probably still asleep. Everyone in my family likes to push "snooze" until the last possible second. I guess it's a Salinger family trait.

On my way through the kitchen I gave Thurber a dog biscuit. Then I headed toward the first-floor bathroom, humming the Mozart sonata I had been performing in my dream. I was already picturing the frozen waffles I was going to make myself for breakfast. The thought of maple syrup always wakes me up.

When I got to the bathroom, I almost tripped over my

two-year-old brother. "Owen!" I yelped. "What are you doing?"

Owen looked up at me with his wide blue eyes. He was sitting on the bathroom floor with a roll of toilet paper in his hands.

Correction—it *used* to be a roll of toilet paper. Now only the cardboard center was left. The actual toilet paper was strewn around the bathroom, along with what appeared to be the contents of an entire tube of toothpaste.

The full-length mirror on the door was covered with fluorescent green toothpaste. There was also a trail of toothpaste on the white tile floor . . . leading directly from Owen to my sock-covered feet.

"Bailey?" I called. No answer. "Julia? Charlie?" Still nothing. I walked toward my little brother, *trying* not to step on toothpaste as I went.

"Where is everybody?" I asked him. "How did you get down here?"

"Joola," Owen answered. I knew what he meant— Julia had brought him downstairs from his room. But where was she?

I picked up Owen. He immediately stuck his toothpaste-covered hands into my hair. Great. Now I had to take a shower before school.

I carried Owen over to the stairs. "Hellooo!" I yelled at the top of my lungs.

4

My eighteen-year-old brother, Bailey, appeared at the top of the stairs. "We're all up here, Claud," he called.

"Owen just created a natural disaster in the bathroom," I said. But Bailey didn't even hear me. He'd already disappeared.

"Bay uptairs," Owen said in his two-year-old talk. He pointed to the staircase.

I started up the steps. "Yep, that's Bailey," I said to Owen, hugging him close to my hip. Even covered with toothpaste, he was cute. "Can you say 'Bailey'?"

"Bay," he said again. Oh, well. "That's okay, Owen. Everyone else calls him Bay too," I told my brother.

We reached the second floor, and I set Owen down. He headed directly for Charlie's room.

Charlie, Julia, and Bailey were all in there. Charlie was flipping through a stack of papers, muttering to himself. Julia stood next to Mom's desk, opening and shutting drawers. Bailey sat at Dad's desk, frowning at Charlie.

"What's going on?" I asked.

Charlie glanced up from the papers. "Trouble, Claudia. Big trouble."

I looked toward Bailey for further explanation. Out of all my family, he's the one who takes the most time to explain things to me. But today all he could do was shake his head. "Nothing for you to worry about, Claud," he said.

But I could tell from the look on his face that there *was* something to worry about. "Well, can I do anything?" I asked.

Julia turned from the desk. "Clean up Owen. He's a mess."

*Tell me something I don't know,* I thought. But I picked him up again. Whatever they were upset about, they didn't want to tell me.

"Bath time, Owen," I said. By the time I got him clean, I would barely have time to brush my teeth— much less make frozen waffles.

"Looks like I'm going to have to eat a cold Pop-Tart for breakfast," I said to no one in particular. "Again."

"Sure, Claudia, whatever you want," Julia responded. But she wasn't even looking at me. She was staring at a piece of paper and frowning.

With Owen in my arms I slipped quietly out of the room.


"Hey, Claudia!" I heard my best friend, Jody Lynch, shout.

I turned around. "What?"

"Do you dare me to go up to Mr. Grodinski and tell him he has spinach in his teeth?" Jody nodded toward the eighth-grade biology teacher. For the record, he's better known as Mr. *Gross*inski. I rolled my eyes.

Jody and I were hanging out in front of Walt Whitman Junior High during our fifteen-minute break between third and fourth periods (they quit calling it "recess" after sixth grade). Every two minutes Jody suggested a dumb prank we could pull to add some excitement to our free time.

"He doesn't have spinach in his teeth," I pointed out.

Jody shrugged. "You have no imagination." She flipped her reddish shoulder-length hair over one shoulder and stared at a crowd of eighth-grade boys who were standing a few yards away.

"I also have no interest in wallpapering my locker with detention slips," I responded. Jody gets at least one detention every day.

"Suit yourself, Fiddle Girl."

Jody has been calling me Fiddle Girl practically since the first day we met. The nickname fits pretty well— my violin usually isn't more than a few feet from my side.

"Thanks. I will." I turned back around and continued to read the flyer I had been studying.

*Three, two, one* . . . I counted down mentally. Jody is naturally curious—okay, *nosy*. I knew she'd want to see what I was reading.

"What's that?" she asked right on schedule. She peered over my shoulder and squinted her eyes.

"Some flyer for an eighth-grade mixer this weekend," I said casually. Jody usually makes fun of any activity that's even slightly related to school. So I didn't want to admit that the mixer actually sounded like fun to me.

She nudged me out of the way and moved closer to the wall. "Come to the Mingle Madness Mixer with the rest of your eighth-grade classmates," Jody read aloud. "Saturday at the gym. Eight o'clock P.M."

I waited for her to make fun of the mixer, but she just looked thoughtfully at the flyer for a few more seconds. "Sounds cool," she said finally. "We don't have anything else to do Saturday night."

I raised my eyebrows. "You're volunteering to be on school property when it's not required? Are you sure you feel okay?" I teased her.

Jody and school don't go together. At all. Jody's idea of school spirit is putting Saran Wrap over the toilets in the girls' room. And she's so used to having detention after school that sometimes she accidentally goes even when she doesn't have to.

"This dance could be the most important party of the year." Jody smiled and moved her gaze to the group of boys. "Need I say more?" she asked.

Lately Jody has become more interested in meeting boys than in putting glue or thumbtacks on teachers' chairs. "You really think the guys in our class will show up at a mixer?" I asked.

"Of course," Jody said. "They want to check us out as much as we want to check them out."

I nodded, even though I never thought of myself as the kind of girl who gets "checked out." I mean, lots of guys ask to copy my math homework, but that isn't the same as slow-dancing to Whitney Houston in the gym.

"So, it's settled," Jody continued. "We're going."

I glanced at the flyer again and shook my head. "I can't."

"Why not?" Jody demanded, narrowing her eyes at me.

*"Duh,"* I said. "I've only told you, like, a thousand times that I've got a violin competition this weekend."

Jody is a great friend, but sometimes she gets so caught up in her life that she forgets about the things that are important to me. Like playing the violin.

I've been taking violin lessons since I was Owen's age. I'm what people call a virtuoso. That means I play really well. I inherited my musical talent from my mother. She was the best violinist I've ever heard—she even played solos with the San Francisco Symphony! Whenever I play, I think of Mom. I even keep her picture in my violin case. If I need inspiration, I just look at that old black-and-white photo.

Anyway, this weekend was one of the biggest competitions of my life—the Northern California Junior Music Championship. It was a really big deal. It was being held at this huge college, the University of California at Berkeley. The competition was spread over two days:

one round on Saturday afternoon, the second round on Saturday night, and the finalists' round on Sunday morning. I couldn't wait!

"Can't you blow off the contest?" Jody asked.

I shook my head. My violin teacher, Ross, had been training me for the competition for months. And I could never let him down. Ross isn't only my teacher, he's also my friend. Besides, my brothers and sister were probably planning some kind of celebration party for after the competition. Everyone was looking forward to it.

"No way," I told Jody.

"Not even to meet cute guys?" Jody asked.

"I can't," I said firmly. "Too many people are counting on me to win. Besides, I need the money."

Jody looked interested. "Money?"

"If I win the violin competition, I get scholarship money for music camp next summer," I explained. *"Plus* a hundred dollars in cash right now."

Jody sighed. "You're crazy, Claudia. You'll be a social outcast if you miss this mixer," she declared. "How will you ever meet any boys?"

"I'm already a social outcast," I responded. Which wasn't totally true. I mean, I have plenty of friends. But I don't think I'll ever be the popular type. I don't think I'll ever even fit into any type at all.

I guess that's why Jody is my best friend. She's not a type either.

"You act like such a nerd sometimes," Jody said, shaking her head.

"Yeah, right." I laughed.

"I'm not kidding, Claudia. I've had enough," Jody said. "I just can't hang out with you anymore."

# chapter two

My jaw dropped open. Was Jody serious? Was she really going to stop hanging out with me?

"Gotcha!" Jody exclaimed. "I was only joking, Claud."

I felt my cherry Pop-Tart settle back down in my stomach.

Jody gave me a light punch in the arm. "It's just a school dance. No big deal."

"You're not mad?" I wanted to be sure.

"Hey, you're the original Fiddle Girl. You *have* to go to the competition."

"Besides, you can go with Caroline and Tiffany to the mixer," I said.

"Yeah, whatever," Jody answered. "We've got more important things to think about."

"Like what?" I asked.

*"Hello.* The hundred bucks." Jody pushed her fingers together and cracked her knuckles. She always does that when she's excited. "What are your chances of winning?"

"Are you kidding?" I said. "I'm a sure thing. I've never lost a violin competition."

Jody slung one of her arms around my shoulders. "In that case, let's start planning."

"Planning what?"

"The awesome time we're going to have with *your* hundred smackeroos," she said.

"We'll start with an all-you-can-eat buffet at PJ's Pancakes," I suggested.

"Then we'll sneak into an R-rated movie at the Haight Odeon," Jody continued.

I was glad Jody understood how important the violin is to me. But something was still bothering me.

How would I ever grow up to be a normal teenager if I was always off playing the violin? On Saturday night the other girls in my class would be dancing and finding boyfriends. And I'd be by myself playing classical music for a bunch of old people.

I could imagine the gym decorated for the mixer. The bright gym lights would be dimmed. Streamers and balloons would hang from the high ceiling. There might even be a fog machine. And a band. I could almost hear the music playing. Not violin music either.

And where would I be? Standing on a lonely stage, wearing a boring, uncomfortable dress. Sure, I'd be playing a beautiful piece of music. But I'd be missing something great.

"And then we'll go to the Haight and watch the hippies tell stories about the sixties," I heard Jody saying.

I nodded, but my mind was still at the mixer. What would happen if I *did* blow off the competition?

Then I thought of Julia, Bailey, and Charlie. Even Owen. My family is ultra-into my violin playing. If I didn't go to the competition, they would be really disappointed.

And I didn't want to let them down. Not even for a night with my friends.

I was humming Korngold's Concerto for Violin in D as I walked into Salinger's at six-thirty. I had to decide between playing that or Mozart's Violin Sonata in G at the competition—I love both pieces. Maybe some pasta primavera would help me with the decision.

I took a deep breath. The smell of tomato sauce and garlic made my stomach rumble. I was starved. At school we'd had the option of turkey surprise or mushy ravioli for lunch. Yuck.

I should probably explain what Salinger's means to our family. It was our dad's restaurant—he used to own it with his best friend, Joe. When I was little, Dad would take me back to the kitchen. He would let me pour hot fudge onto the sundaes being made for customers.

I walked quickly toward a row of booths along the back wall. Charlie, Bailey, Julia, and Owen were already sitting in our usual booth. I barely had to look where I was going. I've wound my way through the tables at Salinger's so many times, I could probably do it blind-folded.

Now that my dad is gone and Joe is retired, Charlie manages Salinger's. At first he hated the job. But now I think he kind of likes it. Charlie redecorated the whole restaurant—he even planned a new menu. The restaurant is doing better than ever.

After our parents died, all of us kids had a million meetings to talk about who should do what. You know—family responsibilities now that Mom and Dad were gone. But the meetings usually ended in disaster—Bailey would yell at Charlie, Charlie would yell at Julia, Owen would just yell in general. Babies are like that. But something good came out of at least one family fight-fest. We promised that we would all eat dinner together at Salinger's at least once a week. Tonight was one of those nights.

"Hey," I said, approaching the booth. I squeezed past

Owen's high chair and slid into the booth next to Bailey.

Julia, Charlie, and Bailey seemed to be involved in some deep conversation. Owen was banging a spoon on the tray of his high chair. I don't think any of them even noticed I'd arrived.

"Hello," I repeated.

Charlie stopped talking. "Oh, hi, Claud," he said.

Bailey moved over a little to give me more room in the booth. "Hi."

"How was school?" Julia asked as she began making funny faces at Owen.

"School was fine," I said. "There's going to be a mixer—" I stopped talking when I saw Bailey nod at Charlie, then glance at me. Something was up.

"Hey, what were you guys talking about?" I asked.

"Nothing," Bailey answered quickly.

"Yeah, nothing," Julia said. She picked up a menu.

Sometimes they act as if I'm an idiot. We've all memorized the menu at least five times over. Well, except for Owen—but he can't even read. "I *know* you guys were talking about something. Your mouths were moving and sound was coming out."

"We weren't talking about anything you'd be interested in, Claud," Charlie said.

"So, what are you going to eat, Jules?" Bailey asked.

Julia frowned at the menu. "Uh, Caesar salad with grilled chicken," she said.

Charlie nodded. "Good choice."

My brothers and sister can really drive me crazy sometimes. They think just because I'm only twelve, I don't have a brain. But I could tell something was wrong. They were worried.

"I'm a part of this family too," I said. "I have a right to know what's going on."

Bailey started to say something, but Charlie interrupted. "She's right, Bay."

"Thank you." I shot a look at Bailey. He shrugged.

"It's about our taxes," Julia said. She pushed the menu away, frowning.

Ugh. Taxes again. I'll never forget the confusion our house was in last April. Bailey had been pestering Charlie for weeks about doing the taxes. And Charlie told Bailey a hundred times that he was totally on top of it. But Charlie's idea of being "on top" of the taxes was having a few shoe boxes full of receipts.

Bailey wanted to hire an accountant, but Charlie refused. He said, and I quote: "Why pay some suit-wearing, overeducated geek to do what every American citizen should be able to do for himself—or herself?"

So Charlie, Julia, and Bailey ended up filling out our tax forms the night they were due. I learned a lot of new bad words that night. The three of them sat at the kitchen table with calculators for *hours*. Then we all drove to the downtown post office at 11:58 P.M., two minutes before the midnight deadline. On the way home from the post office, Charlie promised that next year he would hire an accountant.

"I thought we *did* our taxes," I said.

"We did," Bailey answered. "But we messed up."

"Thanks to Charlie," Julia muttered.

"Julia—" Charlie started to say.

I held up my hands. "Just tell me what's going on."

"We're being audited," Charlie said. "It can happen to anyone."

"What does that mean?" I asked.

"We might not have paid enough money for our taxes," Bailey explained. "Thanks to Charlie's creative mathematics."

"Hey, you're the one who was adding up all our receipts," Charlie responded.

"Only because *you* wouldn't hire an accountant," Julia told Charlie.

I wished I'd never asked what they were talking about. Taxes are boring with a capital B.

"I'm pretty excited about my competition this weekend," I said to change the subject. *Except for the fact that I'm missing the social event of the season,* I added silently.

"Jules, you're the one who insisted we could take a deduction for that huge plumbing bill," Bailey said.

"Excuse me, Mr. They'll-never-audit-nobodies-like-us," Julia snapped. "I didn't hear you arguing about it last April."

"The competition is this weekend. I need to be there by two o'clock on Saturday," I said loudly. "Who's going to drive me?"

Nobody heard me. At least, nobody answered. I took a piece of bread from the basket and began eating. I gave Owen a little bit too.

"So when *exactly* is the auditor coming?" Bailey asked Charlie.

"Saturday afternoon."

Owen threw his bread at Julia. Everyone turned to stare at him. Finally something got their attention!

"Do you think I should buy a new dress for the competition?" I asked quickly.

Julia looked thoughtful. "Well—"

"Claud, we don't have time to talk about a dress right now," Charlie interrupted.

"It's, like, a two-second conversation," I pointed out. "I say 'Should I buy a new dress?' And you guys answer yes or no."

"We'll talk about the dress later," Julia promised. "Okay?"

"Can we at least figure out who's going to take me to the competition?" I asked. Unlike my brothers and sister, I like to be prepared. I'm the kind of person who actually does her homework in study hall.

"Don't worry, Claudia. Either Bailey or I will make absolutely sure that you get to the competition on time," Charlie said.

"Yeah," Bailey added. "And we'll personally inform the judges that if you don't win, they'll have to answer to us!"

"But right now we need to focus on the fact that we're being audited," Charlie said.

"The audit is *boring*," I complained.

"What happened to being a member of the family?" Charlie asked. "I thought you wanted to be in on the discussion."

"I just don't get what the big deal is," I said. "So we messed up some math problems. How much money can we owe?"

Julia bit her lip. "Claud, it's not the money that we're worried about."

I looked around the table. Everyone but Owen was incredibly tense. A sort of hollow feeling grew in the pit of my stomach. "What *are* you worried about?" I asked. I held my breath as I waited for Julia to answer.

"If we really made a mess of the tax forms, and the

government sees we're on our own, then maybe they'll think we're not responsible enough," Julia said softly.

Now my stomach was doing cartwheels. "And . . . ?" I didn't want to hear the answer, but I knew I had to.

Julia put her hand lightly on my arm. "The IRS could contact social services about us."

Suddenly I wasn't hungry anymore. I was glad I hadn't mentioned how disappointed I was about missing the mixer. My brothers and sister had a lot more important stuff to worry about.

I knew what social services could do if they wanted to. They could take Owen and me away from Charlie and give us new guardians. They could send us to foster homes.

They could split up my whole family.

# chapter three

"Yo, Salinger! Think fast," Carin McClain shouted the next afternoon.

*Not again,* I thought. But it was too late. The basketball whizzed toward me. I'd already dropped the ball three times since gym class started. I didn't want to let this one go.

I held out my hands. And caught the ball—with my stomach. "Oomph," I groaned.

"Give it up, Claud," Jody called from the sideline. "You stink."

I tossed the ball to Tiffany Goldman. Jody was right. I stank. Tiffany caught the ball easily. I watched her dribble down the court. Then I limped toward Jody. I was still out of breath from my collision with the basketball.

"Had enough?" Jody asked.

"I'm just taking a break," I panted.

Jody pulled a nail file out of the pocket of her gym shorts. "You need a permanent break, Claud."

"I'm not *that* bad," I insisted.

True, I was one of the shortest girls in our class. When girls like Mia Randall (who is at least five feet six) wanted to keep the ball away from me, all she had to do was hold it high above her head. But at least I tried.

"Why isn't Ms. Hughes making you play?" I asked Jody.

Jody ran the file over her thumbnail. "I told her I had cramps."

Jody amazed me. She'd say *anything* to get out of gym. Both of us had gotten our periods for the first time in the last few months. But I'd rather die than go up to Ms. Hughes and tell her I had *cramps*.

"You're nuts," I said.

Jody smiled and moved the file to the nail of her index finger. "Thanks."

Behind me a whistle blew. "Claudia, back in the game," Ms. Hughes commanded.

"Talk to you later," I told Jody.

I walked to the opposite side of the court, as far away from the ball as I could get. I was actually glad to get back in the game though. As long as I could concentrate on *not* having to catch the basketball again, I wouldn't have time to think about the audit.

Since last night I hadn't been able to get the IRS out of my mind. What would happen if they really tried to split up our family? The thought of going to live in some foster home made me want to throw up.

I stood next to Teri Packard. Even though Teri is tall, she's even worse at basketball than I am. For a few seconds we watched Caroline Suh. Caroline grabbed the ball from Tiffany and went in for a lay-up.

"Are you going to the mixer this weekend?" Teri asked just as Caroline's shot swished through the basket.

"I can't," I answered. "I've got the competition."

"Oh, right," Teri answered. "That will be cool."

Teri plays the flute in the school band. She's probably the only one of my school friends who really understands how important the violin is to me—except Jody.

"I just hope I win."

"You will," Teri assured me.

Ms. Hughes blew her whistle again. "Time to hit the locker room, girls," she shouted.

"Another successful gym period," Teri joked as we walked toward the locker room. "I didn't have to shoot a single basket!"

24

Jody fell into step beside us. She held up her fingernails for Teri and me to inspect. "What do you think?" Jody asked. "Are these babies gorgeous or what?"

"They look great," Teri said. "What's the occasion?"

"The mixer," Jody answered, pushing open the locker room door.

"What about the mixer?" Caroline asked. Caroline was in the middle of changing from her blue and red gym suit to the flowered minidress she'd worn to school. I noticed that the word "training" didn't belong in front of her bra. Unlike me, Caroline has actual breasts.

Jody held up her fingernails. "I gave myself a manicure. All the better to run my fingers through Cory Jacobson's hair while we're slow-dancing Saturday night."

I saw Caroline and Tiffany glance at each other. "Jody's really wild," Teri whispered to me.

I shrugged. Jody likes to talk big. But she doesn't really know that much more about boys than I do. Okay, she knows *some* more. But she's no expert.

I spun the combination of my locker. I couldn't wait to take off my gym suit. The T-shirt smelled like a mixture of old socks and the Laura Ashley perfume that Julia gave me for my twelfth birthday.

"What about you, Claudia?" Caroline asked. "Are you going to do your nails for the dance?"

"Nope," I said. "But I might do my nails for the violin competition I'll be at while the rest of you are at the mixer." I pulled my jeans and red shirt out of my locker.

"You're not coming to the dance?" Carin asked. She looked up from the argyle sock she was pulling onto her left foot.

"I can't. I'll be at Berkeley, playing the violin," I said proudly. I pulled on my jeans, then bent down to pull on my shoes.

"Ooh. Berkeley." Carin whistled. "College guys."

I rolled my eyes. Why do so many girls have to think about boys all the time? I mean, I like to think about boys—don't get me wrong. But not *all* the time.

I poked my head through the top of my flannel shirt. "I'll be too busy competing to pay much attention to guys."

"Claud's going to hit the jackpot," Jody added. "I'm talking *cash* prize."

"Cool," Tiffany said. She shut her locker door with a bang that echoed through the room.

"Too bad you'll miss the mixer," Carin said to me. "You won't get to see my new dress. It's awesome."

"Oh. Yeah, too bad," I answered. What was I supposed to say?

Caroline took a brush from her locker. "I used to play the violin," she said, running the brush through her long black hair.

"Really?" I was surprised. Caroline is one of the most social people in our class—I couldn't imagine her giving up her free time to practice an instrument.

"Yeah. When I was, like, little," she answered. "But it's pretty weird to play when you're *our* age. I mean, you have to practice so much. Wouldn't you rather go out with your friends or something?"

I could feel my face starting to turn red. "I *do* go out. All the time," I told her. But I was still worried about what Caroline said. Did people really think I was weird? Just because I played an instrument?

Jody glanced up from the button she was fastening on her faded denim overalls. "There's nothing weird about winning a hundred bucks," she declared.

Caroline ran the brush through her hair one more time and tossed it back into her locker. "All I'm saying is that Claudia is going to miss out on a lot if she's always stuck at some boring music recital. It's not normal."

"You don't have to talk about me like I'm not here," I told Caroline.

Caroline raised one eyebrow. "Today you're skipping out on an eighth-grade mixer," she said. "Tomorrow it might be the senior prom."

"The senior prom is hardly tomorrow, Caroline," I snapped. "It's like five years away." But my face was still red, and I felt as if I were going to cry or something. I hate arguing with people, especially about the violin. It's really important to me. Even if it made me miss the most important dance of the year.

"Claudia's talent is way more important than the mixer." Jody picked up her backpack and slung it over her shoulder. "Who cares about some stupid junior high dance? Claudia is going to be famous someday."

Caroline shrugged. "Do what you want, Claudia. But you'll never meet any boys if you spend all your time playing violin."

I couldn't believe Caroline! She thought being pretty and popular made her some sort of expert on life.

"Let's go, Jody," I said.

My sneakers made squeaking sounds as we started across the gymnasium floor. For a few seconds neither Jody nor I said anything.

"You stood up for yourself in there, Fiddle Girl," Jody said finally. "I'm proud of you."

"Yeah." I sighed. "I guess I have more important things to worry about than a stupid mixer—or a violin competition."

"Trouble in the Salinger household?" Jody asked.

I shrugged. I didn't want to talk about the tax audit. I wanted to forget I'd ever heard the words.

"Come on, Claud, you can't fool me. What's going on?"

I glanced around the gym. "Can you keep a secret?"

"Can Jody Lynch keep a secret, she asks," Jody said, gazing up at the gym's high ceiling. "The girl wants to know if Jody, Queen of You-tell-you-die, can keep her mouth shut."

Jody was more like the queen of melodrama, but I got her point. I led her to the bleachers that lined one side of the gym. We sat down in the first row. "Our family might get split up," I announced. Just saying it out loud made me sick.

Jody's jaw dropped. "What?" she shrieked. "What do you mean, split up?"

"Shh. The whole school doesn't need to know." I lowered my voice to a loud whisper.

"So, what's the deal?" Jody whispered back.

"The IRS is out to get us," I explained. "We're being audited."

"The Internal Revenue Service?" Jody gasped. Her eyes looked like they were about to drop out of her head.

"Are they that bad?" Now I was really scared! Jody

was usually totally casual about anything that had to do with authority.

"They can ruin your life like *that.*" Jody snapped her fingers.

"Really? How do you know?" I leaned forward and put my elbows on my shaky knees.

"Oh, man. There's this friend of my dad's, right?"
I nodded.

"He didn't pay his taxes for, like, five years. So one day he gets a letter from the IRS."

I nodded again. "Just get to the end."

"After he got audited . . . he ended up going to jail for a whole year!"

*"Jail?"* I imagined myself behind bars. I'd wear one of those black and white striped outfits. For breakfast, lunch, and dinner I'd have nothing but bread and water. And tall girls—basketball players—would probably beat me up.

"But I'm sure that won't happen to you guys," Jody said. She glanced at the big clock on the wall of the gym. "Oops. Got to run. If I'm late for history one more time, Mr. Chandler's going to stick me with a week of detention."

I wanted to ask Jody a million more questions about her dad's friend. But she was already standing up and swinging her backpack across her shoulders.

"See ya later, Claud," Jody said over her shoulder.

"Wait—"

Jody kept walking. "Don't worry, Claudia," she yelled. "If they throw you in the slammer, I'll bring you a cake with a file baked into it."

I tried to smile. "Thanks, Jody. I feel a lot better now."

I slouched on the bench, watching Jody hurry toward the huge red steel doors on the other side of the gym. I knew Jody was exaggerating. I mean, there was no way Charlie could go to jail for a simple mistake. Right?

I didn't feel ready to go to English class. One late slip wouldn't kill me. I closed my eyes. Maybe if I went over Beethoven's Concerto for Violin in my head, I'd be able to block out the audit.

*Ba da da da . . .*

"Hey, Claudia!" A boy's voice interrupted the opening notes of the piece.

My eyes flew open. "Oh, hi, Jeff."

"Don't sound so excited to see me," he joked.

Jeff Bloch is one of my closest friends. He's cute, with blond hair and warm brown eyes. But we've known each other so long that I'd never think of him as a boyfriend or anything. I mean, dating him would be about as exciting as a slow dance with one of my brothers. Jeff and I have been friends since second grade, when the Blochs moved into our neighborhood.

"Sorry, I'm just worried about something."

"What?" Jeff asked.

I didn't feel like hearing another story about somebody going to jail for messing up their taxes. "I don't want to talk about it."

"Okay." Jeff isn't one of those people who pries and pries until a person finally spills her guts. He's pretty good at knowing when to talk and when to shut up. When my parents died, he was practically the only person who didn't make me feel like a freak—I didn't hear him whisper the word "orphan" once.

"What are you doing in here anyway?" I asked. "Don't you have art this period?"

"Decorations for the mixer." Jeff pointed to a corner of the gymnasium. Mrs. Wilensky's sixth-period art class drifted into the gym, holding streamers, paper lanterns, and construction paper cutouts.

Pete Hennesey climbed onto a ladder, holding up one end of a large banner. In my opinion, Pete is one of the cutest boys in the eighth-grade class. He's got this big pile of red hair, and his smile is so wide that people tell him he looks like Bozo the Clown. But I like his smile. He waved, and I waved back.

"Jeff, we need you over here," Mrs. Wilensky yelled from the other side of the room.

"Duty calls," Jeff said.

I picked up my backpack. "I'd better go too. I'm supposed to be in English."

We walked side by side until we reached the middle of the gym. "See ya, Claud," Jeff said. He headed toward the rest of the kids.

"Bye." I started to jog toward the double steel doors. Now that I was finally on my way to class, I began to picture Mr. Schiller's face when I walked into English ten minutes late.

*I got locked in the girls' bathroom. I sprained my ankle on the stairs. I had to dig through the trash for my retainer.* As I reached the exit, I tried out different excuses for being late. *I was upset because social services might take me away from my family.*

I propped the door open with my foot, then turned to look at the art class. They had already put up a large red banner: WELCOME, EIGHTH-GRADERS. I gave the banner ten points for color and one point for originality.

There were also purple, pink, and green streamers hanging from the walls. Definitely ten points for cheesy. Still, I thought the decorations were kind of pretty.

Pete jumped down from the ladder he'd been standing on. "What do you think, Claudia?" he shouted.

"Looks great," I yelled back.

He gave me one of his huge smiles and my heart began to pound. "See you at the mixer!" he called.

I slipped out the door. The heavy metal banged shut behind me.

*No you won't,* I answered silently.

# chapter four

"Hi, Ross," I greeted my violin teacher after school.

"Hey, Claud." Ross stepped away from the front door of his apartment.

Ross is really great. He's got blond hair and blue eyes that twinkle from behind his glasses. He also gives me violin lessons free. Since our family has to spend a lot of money on day care for Owen, we would have a hard time paying for music lessons. And Ross is almost a part of the family, so he helps us out by giving me a "scholarship."

I tossed my backpack on an old couch. "Let's get to work," I announced.

"Great. But you might want to take your violin out of its case first." He sat down in his favorite chair.

"Oh. Right." I put my violin case on top of Ross's piano and flipped open the top.

I ran my hand over the smooth wood of the instrument. I wanted to have a great practice today. The competition was only two days away. I lifted the violin, enjoying the familiar weight of the instrument in my hands.

"Ready?" Ross asked.

"Almost." I pulled the photograph of Mom from my violin case and propped it up against the top of the case. "Ready," I said to Ross.

"Let's start with the Mozart," Ross instructed.

I put my violin on my shoulder. Even before my bow hit the strings, I was thinking of the notes of Mozart's Violin Sonata in G. I closed my eyes and started to play. . . .

Mozart's music flowed from my brain to my arm to my fingertips to the strings of my violin. As I played note after note, the thoughts that had been crowding my head all day dissolved into the air around me.

I finished the piece and glanced at Ross. He clapped. "Excellent, Claud. You'd make Mozart proud."

"Thanks." Ross's praise means a lot to me. I mean, Julia, Bailey, and Charlie are always telling me that my pieces sound great. But they don't know much about classical music. And since Mom died, their taste has gone *way* downhill.

But Ross knows his stuff. And he's always honest with me. If my playing is bad, he'll come right out and tell me I haven't been practicing enough.

"The Mozart and the Korngold are both in good shape," Ross continued. "So which one are you going to play this weekend?"

I shook my head. "I can't choose. I like them both."

Ross took off his glasses. "Which one does Charlie think you should play?" he asked as he wiped the lenses with the bottom of his shirt.

"Charlie hasn't said *anything* about the competition."

Ross slipped his glasses back on his nose. "He hasn't forgotten about it, has he?"

"No. He's just got a lot on his mind." I flopped on Ross's couch. Even though the stuffing is coming out, the sofa is mega comfortable. I rested my violin on my chest.

"Why? Is something going on down at the restaurant?"

I groaned. "No, our taxes are being audited," I explained. I always tell Ross what's going on at home. He's practically another big brother to me, so I figure he can hear about our family problems.

"Charlie, Bailey, and Julia don't have time to worry about anything but receipts and tax forms," I said. *And the fact that our family may be split up,* I added to myself.

"That's tough," Ross said.

"And . . ."

"What?" he prompted.

"Nothing. It's just this dumb mixer at school." I didn't know why I was even bringing up the mixer. I wasn't going. Period. End of story.

"And what dumb mixer is that?" Ross asked. He leaned back in his chair and folded his hands in his lap. I call that his psychiatrist pose.

"There's a dance for eighth-graders Saturday night," I said.

"Ah-ha! And you can't go because of this competition."

I laid my violin on the floor and rolled over on my stomach. "Everybody else will be there," I muttered into one of the big pillows at the end of the couch. "The *normal* people who don't play instruments."

"Who's everybody?"

I turned my head to the side so I could look at Ross. "What do you mean, who's everybody?" I asked. Thinking of the mixer was making me cranky. *"Everybody* is everybody. Jody, Caroline, Teri, Tiffany, Jeff, Pete—"

Ross laughed. "Everybody," he concluded.

I sat up on the couch and picked up my violin again. "Hey, Ross?"

"What?"

"Do you think it's strange that I want to play the violin all the time?"

He frowned. "Why do you ask?"

"Caroline Suh told me that I was weird because I waste my time practicing violin. She said I might end up missing the senior prom."

Ross moved over to the sofa and sat down next to me. I knew I was in for a lecture. Whenever Ross wants to get serious, he makes sure he can look directly into my eyes.

"Claudia, mastering a musical instrument takes a lot of sacrifice," he began. "Sometimes it *would* be more fun to go to a party or out for pizza with your friends than to stay home and do scales on the violin."

"I sense a 'but' coming," I said. Ross gives great advice. But if I don't hurry him up, he tends to go on and on.

He gave me a look that went straight through my eyes and into my skull. *"But* the payoff is huge. Caroline Suh might have a good time at the mixer, *but* she doesn't have an enormous talent that she can share with people." He paused. "You do."

"Oh, yeah. Talent." I sighed. Ross was right. Mom always told me that my talent was important. But I hated being so *different* all the time. Just because I had this so-called musical gift, I had to spend all my time practicing.

Ross grinned. "Feel better?"

I shrugged. "Sort of."

"Good. Because I want to hear that Korngold. Until you decide which piece to perform at Berkeley, you've got to practice both. And you've got only one more day until the moment of truth."

I sighed and dragged myself off the couch. Then I lifted my violin and began to play.

"So, am I ready?" I asked Ross an hour later. I moved the photograph of my mom to the bottom of my case, then put my violin on top of it.

"Getting there," Ross said. "But you really need to decide which piece to play."

"I know, I know. I'll make up my mind tonight," I promised.

"Mmm. Okay." Ross was leafing through a pile of sheet music. I wasn't sure he had even heard what I said. I decided to test him.

"I think I'm on fire," I said casually. "My clothes are burning up."

"Good, Claud," Ross responded.

I put my hands on my hips. "Geez, Ross. You don't need to ignore me just because my lesson is over."

He glanced up from the pile of music and grinned. "Sorry. I have a student coming in any minute. I want to make sure I've got her music in front of me."

*"Who?"* Usually I was the last student Ross taught on Thursdays.

The doorbell rang. "You can meet her yourself, right now," he answered.

When he opened the door, I saw a girl about my age. She had long blond hair and the kind of blue eyes that old ladies ooh and aah over. A woman holding a violin case stood next to her.

"Good afternoon, Ross," the woman said. "We're ready for our lesson." She sounded like one of those perfect TV moms.

Ross placed a sheet of music on top of the piano. "Terrific." He turned to me. "Claudia Salinger, meet Sabrina Monteclaire and her mother. They just moved up here from Los Angeles."

"Hi," I said. I was pretty sure that Sabrina was my age, but I hadn't seen her around school. Judging from the size of the diamond studs in her ears, I figured she probably went to a private school across the bay in Sausalito.

"Hello, Claudia," Mrs. Monteclaire answered. She reached out and shook my hand. "It's always a pleasure to meet one of Ross's students."

"Nice to meet you," Sabrina said. She sounded shy.

"Are you entered in the competition this weekend, Claudia?" Mrs. Monteclaire asked.

I nodded. "Yeah."

Mrs. Monteclaire smiled warmly. "How wonderful. So is Sabrina."

"She is?" I asked. I turned to her. "I mean, you are?" I was surprised. I had no idea that Ross had any other students in the competition. I thought *I* was the only one good enough to make it. Sabrina must be a great violin player.

Sabrina nodded. "Yes. But I don't have a chance of winning."

Mrs. Monteclaire wrapped her arm around Sabrina's shoulders. "Of course you have a chance, honey," she said.

"Sabrina gets *so* nervous," Mrs. Monteclaire told Ross and me. "But I'll be right there with her this weekend. Cheering her on. And maybe you girls can keep each other company." She smiled at me.

I liked Mrs. Monteclaire. She was such a *mom.* Brothers and sisters are great. But I wished my mother could be at the competition.

I pushed thoughts of Mom out of my head. "You'll be fine," I told Sabrina. "Everybody gets nervous before big competitions."

Ross cleared his throat. "We'd better get started, Sabrina." He turned to me. "See you tomorrow, Claud."

"Go ahead and start," I told Ross. "I just need to put on my jacket."

"I'm so glad we met, Claudia," Mrs. Monteclaire said as Sabrina set down her violin case. "We'll see you on Saturday."

I nodded.

"All right, team. Let's practice," Ross said.

Ross sounded so enthusiastic. Did he like teaching Sabrina more than me? I shook my head. That was impossible. *I* was Ross's favorite student. I was his *friend.*

Sabrina took her violin from its case as her mother sat on the sofa. I headed out to the front hall to get my jean jacket.

"Ross, we've picked out Sabrina's dress for the final round of competition on Sunday," I heard Mrs. Monteclaire say. "It's just adorable."

Sabrina was lucky. She had her own personal cheerleader. At my lessons it's always just me and Ross. Charlie, Bailey, and Julia give me rides back and forth to Ross's apartment as often as they can. But none of them ever comes in.

I began to pull on my jacket as I moved closer to the living room doorway. I wanted to hear the conversation. Listening to Mrs. Monteclaire talk reminded me of the old days—when Mom used to come to violin lessons with me.

"I don't think her dress is as important a choice as the music she'll be playing," Ross answered. "What's it going to be?"

"Brahms," Sabrina replied.

"Great!" Ross said. "The Brahms is a piece you could win with."

*Win?* I couldn't believe it! Did Ross really think Sabrina could beat me? I mean, most of the performers were going to be high schoolers. The only reason I was even *accepted* into the competition was that I was so good. Could Sabrina really be as good as I was? Or *better?*

One thing was definite. I couldn't leave Ross's apartment until I heard Sabrina play. My jacket was still hanging off one arm, but I didn't care.

"Go ahead, Sabrina," Mrs. Monteclaire was saying. "Show Ross how much you've improved."

For a moment I imagined that Mrs. Monteclaire's voice was my own mother's. *Go ahead, Claudia. Show Ross how much you've improved.*

Sabrina started to play. I recognized the piece immediately. It was a Brahms I had worked on last fall. I closed my eyes so I could listen to the notes. Sabrina's playing sounded a little hesitant. I breathed a sigh of relief. Nothing to worry about.

I pulled my denim jacket on the rest of the way. Ross didn't really think Sabrina could win the competition. He was just being nice.

I put my hand on the doorknob. Bailey was probably waiting outside in the car for me.

Then I froze.

Suddenly the music coming from the living room didn't sound hesitant. It sounded . . . well, good. Okay, great. Sabrina was playing the Brahms piece as well as I could. If not better.

I yanked open the door. I wanted to get out of Ross's apartment as fast as possible. I needed to get home and practice. Sure, Sabrina wasn't any real competition. Her piece was much easier than either one I was thinking of. But she wasn't my only competition either.

I raced down the two flights of stairs to the front door. Mozart or Korngold? Korngold or Mozart? The question turned over and over in my mind.

I needed a second opinion.

Outside, Bailey was double-parked. I ran over and pulled open the car door. Bailey had the stereo blasting. He was listening to an Oasis song, banging his hands against the steering wheel in time to the music.

" 'Save me. When you gonna saaave me,' " Bailey

wailed along with the lead singer of Oasis. He was totally off-key. The phrase "tone-deaf" came to mind.

"Hi," I shouted over the music. I put my violin case on the backseat and climbed into the car.

"How was practice?" Bailey asked.

"Interesting," I said.

I waited for him to ask why practice was interesting. But he didn't.

Bailey continued to bang on the steering wheel. "Seat belt," he said. Like he needed to remind me. Since my parents' accident, I always wear my seat belt.

"I *know*," I said. I clicked the seat belt into place.

"What took you so long anyway?" Bailey asked over the noise of the song.

I brightened. "Well, Ross had this new student. She's my age. And she's really good. She made me realize that I really need to practice . . . anyway, it's kind of a long story."

"I hope you don't need to make any stops," Bailey said. I guess he didn't care what the long story was. " 'Cause I've got to get home and work on the taxes."

I was beginning to understand the expression my father always walked around muttering around April 15. *The only thing you can depend on in life is death and taxes.* I had definitely experienced more of both than I ever could have imagined.

"You're not the only one with a life, you know," I said. "I need to get home too."

He nodded to the beat. " 'Saaaave me,' " he repeated for the tenth time since I'd gotten in the car.

Bailey pulled into traffic. I leaned forward and turned down the stereo. "Bay?"

He flicked on the blinker. "What, Claud?"

"Which piece do you think I should perform at the competition this weekend? The Mozart? Or the Korngold?"

Bailey cranked up the volume on the Jeep's stereo. "The Oasis!" he shouted.

# chapter five

"So what do you think?" I asked my brother Thursday night. "Mozart or Korngold? And I want a serious answer."

"Cla-dee," Owen answered. He waved his little hands in the air. "Play!"

On most evenings I'd be thrilled that Owen was making such an effort to talk to me. But tonight I just wished he were old enough to know the difference between Mozart and Korngold.

"You're right," I told Owen. "Mozart is definitely the way to go."

"Moo-moo," Owen replied. He bounced up and down on the sofa. "Play!"

"Okay! You've convinced me. I'll do the Mozart." I handed Owen a few wooden blocks, which I hoped would keep him busy. "I'm glad we've cleared that up," I continued.

Owen nodded as if he actually understood what I was talking about. "Cla-dee play blocks?"

I shook my head. "Cla-dee has to practice now," I explained. "You play with your blocks."

Owen picked up a block and waved it up and down. I waved my violin bow up and down in response, and Owen giggled.

I'm used to baby-sitting for my little brother. Owen goes to day care, and sometimes we hire baby-sitters—but there's still a lot of time when the family has to pitch in and take care of him.

We've ended up in some pretty funny situations. One time Bailey had to take Owen to football practice. Another time Julia took him to school with her. Tonight I had baby-sitting duty.

Charlie, Bailey, and Julia were still in a panic over the audit on Saturday. They were all in the kitchen with calculators and the adding machine. Charlie even had a pencil stuck behind his ear. And he hadn't shaved for at least two days.

Meanwhile Julia was completely losing her mind. That afternoon she found a pay receipt that Charlie hadn't included in our tax forms. I don't really understand the details, but I guess finding the receipt was bad. Very bad.

I patted Owen on the head. "Moo-moo," he said again.

I smiled at him. "Since everybody else is busy, I'll play the Mozart for you," I told Owen.

He clapped his hands. This was good. Maybe my little brother was going to turn out to enjoy classical music more than Charlie, Bailey, and Julia did.

I put my violin on my shoulder, then raised my bow. I kept one eye glued to Owen. The other eye strayed to the picture of Mom in my violin case.

I took a deep breath and began the piece. I moved the bow up and down the strings of my violin, faster and faster. The music was flowing through me. . . .

"Ouch," I yelped. I dropped my bow and rubbed my head. Owen had thrown a block. And the block made a direct hit—on my head!

"I guess you don't like the Mozart after all," I said. Owen wanted to play. I would never be able to practice now. What was I going to do?

I put down my violin. Then I crouched in front of him so I could look him in the eye. "Owen, we need to have a talk," I said in my most grown-up voice.

Owen held out his arms. I reached over and pulled him into my lap.

"I'd love to play blocks with you. I really would. But I've got this big competition this weekend. I *have* to practice."

"Moo," Owen said, snuggling close to me.

"Right, moo," I responded. "Can I practice?"

But Owen didn't say anything. Not even "moo" or "Cla-dee." His eyes were drooping and his head was resting against my shoulder.

"Now we're getting somewhere," I whispered.

I stood up with Owen tucked into my arms. Then I laid him carefully on the couch. "Close your eyes, Owen," I said quietly.

I picked up my violin and bow and began to play "Rock-a-Bye Baby." As my bow slid over the strings, I glanced at Mom's photo. When I was little she tucked me into bed every night. First we would read a story together. My favorite was *Mike Mulligan and the Steam Shovel*. Then she would take out her violin and play lullabies until I fell asleep.

I watched my little brother suck his thumb as he nodded off. I hoped he felt as safe and loved right now as I did when Mom played me to sleep.

"And down will come baby, cradle and all." I finished the song. The room became quiet. I tiptoed over to Owen and leaned close. His chest was moving up and down in a steady rhythm. Perfect. He was sound asleep.

"Now for a little Mozart," I announced, pretending the living room was Carnegie Hall.

I closed my eyes for a moment. I wanted to gather all

my concentration. In less than forty-eight hours I had to play this piece onstage at Berkeley. If I wanted to win the music camp scholarship, I had to be perfect.

I began to play. Once again the notes came easily. My fingers moved up and down. The music rose, then fell.

I smiled as I began the most difficult part of the piece. I'd had trouble with this section before, but I was determined to get the notes right this time.

I lifted the bow just a tiny bit, then let it rest again on the strings—

"Claudia!" Julia yelled from the kitchen.

I kept moving the bow. Didn't she know I was in the middle of something important? And that her yelling could wake up Owen?

"Claudia!" Julia yelled again.

I missed my note. The violin made a screeching sound. Owen's eyes popped open. His face scrunched up and his cheeks turned bright red. I knew what was coming next. He opened his mouth wide . . . and started to scream.

My concentration was gone. Totally destroyed.

"What?" I yelled. Owen's screaming had died down to a loud wail.

"I'm trying to concentrate," Julia called. "Can you take your violin somewhere else?"

I stamped my foot. What did they want me to do?

Take Owen into a closet and play there? "I'm *practicing*," I called. "It's *important.*"

"And figure out what's wrong with Owen," Bailey added. "I've got a huge headache as it is."

I stuck my tongue out in the direction of the kitchen. "He wasn't crying before *someone* woke him up with her loudmouth voice," I muttered.

I tucked my violin and bow under my left arm. With my right arm I scooped up Owen off the sofa.

"Claaa," he cried. His blue eyes were red from crying. Owen was tired and cranky. Not a good combination in a two-year-old.

It's hard to walk with a toddler, a violin, and a bow in your arms. But I managed to make it to the kitchen.

Julia sat at the table with a pad of paper, a pen, and a slice of pepperoni pizza. Charlie was pacing back and forth with a calculator in his hands. Bailey was punching numbers into the adding machine.

"Is everything okay, Claud?" Charlie asked.

I plopped Owen into his high chair and shook out my right arm. Pretty soon my baby brother will be too heavy to pick up!

"No. Everything is not okay. I'm trying to practice for the competition," I said. "And you guys are not helping."

Charlie sighed.

"We're sorry, Claud," Julia said. "We're just really

stressed out." She smiled. "I didn't mean to wake up Owen."

Julia *did* look tired. It seemed like the closer we got to the audit, the more stressed out everyone was getting. I bit my lip. If they were worried, it meant something bad was going to happen when the auditor came.

How could I worry about a competition, when I might lose my brothers and sister?

"I guess we're in big trouble," I said.

"Well, there is some good news." Bailey glanced up from the adding machine.

"Yeah. Charlie *finally* hired an accountant this afternoon," Julia said. "Maybe he can help us out of this mess."

"We'll take care of everything, Claud," Charlie said. "I promise. Don't worry about it."

"Okay," I answered. "Good. Because *I* need to worry about my violin competition."

"Why don't you practice in the basement?" Julia suggested. "You can leave Owen up here."

"The basement?" I asked. Rehearsing in the middle of cobwebs and dusty boxes didn't sound like much fun.

"You know we love your music, Claud," Bailey said. "But right now we really need peace and quiet."

"Fine." I sighed. I bet Sabrina Monteclaire's mother would never make her practice in a dungeon.

"Someone should put Owen to bed soon," I added. "He's really tired."

But nobody was listening to me. They were all back at work on the taxes.

I clomped downstairs to the basement and set up the violin case with Mom's picture. Then I took a deep breath and told myself to concentrate.

I began the Mozart piece. I was only on the third bar when I heard the door at the top of the stairs slam shut.

I couldn't believe it! Bailey, Julia, and Charlie practically locked me down here to practice. They would probably be happier if I didn't practice at all!

I mean, I know how important the audit is. But in my opinion, my brothers and sister didn't seem to care about me or my competition one bit!

So maybe playing the violin isn't all that important, I thought. Maybe I should just go to the mixer instead.

# chapter six

"BaileyJuliaCharlie! I'm home," I yelled.

I was in an awesome mood. It was Friday afternoon, and my practice with Ross had gone *really* well. He thought I was ready to ace the Northern California Junior Music Championship, and so did I. Who needed a junior-high mixer? I was going to have Carnegie Hall!

I threw my backpack onto a chair in the front hall and danced into the living room. "Thank you, thank you," I breathed, bowing to my adoring fans. "The violin is my life!"

"Er, hello there," a voice from the other side of the living room said. I froze mid-bow.

"Uh, hi," I responded, standing up straight. "I, uh, didn't see you there."

A man who looked about the same age as my Grandpa Jake was sitting on the sofa. He wore a charcoal-gray suit and a striped tie.

"I'm Frederick Lemmon," he said. "The accountant."

"Oh. I'm Claudia Salinger." I thought about holding out my hand for him to shake, but I decided not to. Mr. Lemmon didn't look very friendly.

I shifted from one foot to the other, trying to think of something intelligent to say. Mr. Lemmon stared at me as if I were some alien life form.

Suddenly there was a loud crash from the kitchen. I pictured an entire shelf of pots and pans tumbling to the floor. Mr. Lemmon's face grew pale.

"Oops," Bailey called from the kitchen. "Just a little accident. Nothing to worry about."

"Uh, can I get you anything?" I asked the accountant.

He shook his head. "I'm just waiting for your brother to find some rather important documents."

"I know it's around here somewhere!" Bailey shouted. He sounded as if he had been running laps.

Mr. Lemmon gave a loud harrumph.

If Bailey didn't find whatever he was searching for, this accountant would think we were hopeless. As first impressions go, I didn't think we were making a very good one.

"I'm sure Charlie and Bailey have everything in order," I said quickly.

"Really?" Mr. Lemmon looked as if I'd just told him that the world was flat. He tugged on his tie.

I laughed nervously. "Oh, yeah. They're, like, *so* responsible. Responsible is Charlie's middle name. And Bailey's." I laughed again. But it came out sounding more like a bark. "Charlie's our oldest brother, in case you didn't know that. He's down at our restaurant . . . um, being responsible."

*Shut up, Claudia,* I told myself. But I couldn't seem to stop babbling.

"I guess it's a family trait," I continued. "Responsibility, I mean. We all have loads of it. All of us."

Mr. Lemmon kept staring at me as if I were crazy. "Uh, are you sure I can't get you something?" I asked, backing toward the kitchen. "Coffee, tea, Coke? Cold pizza?"

Before I could continue, Bailey darted into the room. His brown hair was a mess, and his face was covered with beads of sweat. He held up a sheet of paper. Well, not an entire sheet. The paper was torn off in several places. "I got it," he declared.

Mr. Lemmon raised his eyebrows. "I see."

Bailey let out a small sound—somewhere between a laugh and a groan. "Yeah, well . . . Thurber sort of got ahold of the document . . ."

Mr. Lemmon raised his eyebrows so high, I thought they would disappear into the small amount of hair on his head. "Thurber?"

"Thurber's our dog," I explained. "He's a bull-dog."

Bailey set the piece of paper on the coffee table in front of Mr. Lemmon. Then he put his hand on my shoulder. "So, you met Claudia."

"I told Mr. Lemmon how *responsible* we are," I said, glancing sideways at Bailey.

"Yes, yes. Very responsible. Everyone says so." Bailey ran the sleeve of his rugby shirt across his forehead.

Mr. Lemmon stared for a moment at the tattered sheet of paper. "It would appear that *everyone* has an interesting definition of the word 'responsible,'" Mr. Lemmon said with a sniff.

Bailey seemed to shrink. I mean it. He's a big guy, but his body actually seemed to get smaller. "Claudia, go do your homework," Bailey commanded.

"Sure," I responded. "Homework." I smiled at Mr. Lemmon and took a step toward the stairs. "Us responsible Salingers. We just love doing our homework."

As I left the living room, I saw Mr. Lemmon frown. I followed his gaze . . . and noticed that he was staring at the half-eaten peanut butter and jelly sandwich I left on the coffee table last night.

I groaned. If the visit from the IRS agent tomorrow was anything like *this* visit, we were in trouble.

Major trouble.

Once I got upstairs, I realized that I didn't even have any homework. I'd finished all my assignments in study hall.

But I *did* need to come up with an outfit for the competition tomorrow. I walked into Charlie's room and flopped on the bed. I tried to picture all my clothes. But I could only think of Sabrina Monteclaire's mother buying her a brand-new dress. I could never compete with a brand-new dress.

Finally I snapped my fingers. "I've got it!"

I would call Jody. After we figured out what I should wear, we could finish plotting exactly how to spend my hundred-dollar prize money. How much more fun did it get?

I grabbed Charlie's phone and dialed the familiar number. One ring. Two rings. Then Jody answered.

"Hi, I need help," I said.

"Hey, Claud," Jody said. "You're lucky I'm home—I just walked in."

"Where were you?" I asked.

"I went shopping with Tiffany and Caroline," she answered. "You know, for mixer dresses."

"Oh." My stomach kind of turned over. Jody was out

shopping with Caroline and Tiffany? Usually she went shopping with me.

"You wouldn't believe what an awesome time we had," Jody went on. "We went to the mall and tried on, like, the most expensive dresses they had. Then we went to Antique Boutique and bought really cool, way cheap black dresses. Mine is really short."

Was Jody ever going to stop and take a breath? She was never this excited about shopping with *me*. Jody must have noticed that I wasn't saying anything.

"Wish you could have been there, Claud," she finally said.

"Maybe I would have been—if you had *invited* me," I answered.

Jody laughed. "I did invite you. At lunch. You said you had practice, remember?"

"Oh. Yeah."

Oops—I was so busy feeling left out that I totally forgot Jody had tried to include me. But that didn't make me feel better. It still seemed weird that my best friend was off shopping and having fun while I was practicing the violin.

"I've to go, Claud," Jody said suddenly. "Mom is calling me."

"Okay. Later."

"By the way, good luck at the competition tomorrow," Jody said.

"Thanks!"

"I'll think of you the whole time Caroline and I are getting our hair cut tomorrow," Jody promised.

She hung up.

The sound of the dial tone made me feel lonely. Between practicing for the competition and worrying about the audit, I hadn't spent any time with Jody for days.

And I still had no idea what I was going to wear to the competition. So much for the good mood I had been in after practice.

I buried my face in Charlie's pillow.

The front door banged shut. A second later I heard the sound of boots clomping up the stairs. Julia! The perfect fashion adviser.

I leapt off Charlie's bed and ran across the hall. "Jules?" I called, knocking lightly on her door. "Can I come in?"

Julia is very big on privacy. I've learned to knock *before* I open the door. Especially if she has a boyfriend over.

The door opened. Julia stepped back a few feet, then twirled around in a circle. "What do you think of this shirt?" she asked.

"Aren't you supposed to be helping Bailey with the accountant?" I asked.

"No," she said. "Bailey is handling it. He's good at

stuff like that. And the baby-sitter is taking care of Owen until Charlie gets home. So I finally have time to think about myself!" Julia turned to the mirror above her dresser and began readjusting the shirt.

I looked at my sister's happy face. Then I thought of the tattered sheet of paper and the grim look on Bailey's face. I wasn't sure Julia was right about Bailey "being good at stuff like that." But I decided to keep my mouth shut. I needed her help.

"So, what do you think?" she asked again.

I scrunched up my face and stared at the shirt for a couple of seconds. "It's sort of boring."

Julia looked down at the shirt, frowning. "Boring? Why?"

"It's all black." She was also wearing black jeans and black boots. Julia looked like she was dressed for a funeral. A *casual* funeral.

Julia twirled again. "Black is sophisticated, Claud. Not boring."

Hmmm. *Black is sophisticated.* I liked the sound of that.

"Do you think I should wear a black dress to the competition?" I asked.

Julia held a red scarf up to her neck. She flicked her long, dark hair over one shoulder. "What?"

I sank onto her bed. "Remember? My violin competition? The event I've been trying to practice for?"

63

Julia turned from the mirror. "Of course I remember, Claud." She draped the scarf over my head and gave me a quick hug. "You're going to be fabulous."

"Not if I have to go *naked*," I muttered through the gauzy material of the scarf.

Julia laughed. "What do you say you and I design the most glamorous outfit we can think of?"

I pulled the scarf off my head. At last! Help was on the way. "I thought you'd never ask."

Julia plopped down next to me on the bed. She leaned back on her elbows and stared into space for a second. "You've got that cute red skirt," she said.

I stuck out my tongue. "I've worn that thing, like, a thousand times."

"How about your plaid kilt?" Julia asked.

"Julia! I got that when I was *ten.*"

Julia nodded. "I guess we haven't gotten you any new dress-up clothes for a while."

"Duh," I said. Was I the only person in the family who paid the least bit of attention to me?

"Well, there must be *something,*" Julia declared. She bounced off the bed. "Let's give your entire wardrobe a once-over."

I slid off the bed. Maybe if I'd gone to the mall with Jody, I wouldn't be in this situation. Maybe I'd have a great new dress to wear.

I started to follow Julia into the hallway.

The phone rang.

"I bet it's Jody calling back. She probably forgot to tell me something," I said to Julia. "You can let the answering machine pick it up."

Julia dodged past me and dove for the phone at the side of her bed. "I'm expecting a call," she said.

Julia picked up the phone on the second ring. "Hello?"

I hummed to myself. I couldn't wait to figure out what I was going to wear.

"Oh, hey," Julia said in this really annoying, whispery voice. "How are you?"

Great, I thought. She was talking to a boy. I can always tell when Julia is on the phone with a guy. Her voice completely changes.

"Five minutes?" Julia asked. A look of panic crossed her face. She glanced at her watch, biting her lip. "No problem."

Julia laughed at something he said. "See you soon." She hung up the phone.

"Ready?" I asked. I turned to go into the hall.

Julia sprinted toward her closet. "Oh, no. Five minutes. How an I going to figure out what to wear in five—"

"Jules!" I interrupted. "Are you going to help me with my outfit, or what?"

"Sorry, Claud," Julia said. "I don't have time." She

continued to flick through every single item in her closet. "I've got to get ready."

"Thanks a lot," I mumbled.

Julia turned around for a second. "I'll help you tomorrow morning, okay?"

"Sure, whatever."

I stomped out of Julia's room and slammed the door behind me. It wasn't fair. My own sister dumped me for a dumb *guy*.

"I guess I *will* go to the competition naked," I muttered.


"Claud, I'm ordering you dinner," Bailey shouted from downstairs.

Huh? I sat up on Charlie's bed. I must have fallen asleep. But I could tell it was dinnertime—I was starved.

I raced down the stairs two at a time. I slid into the kitchen in my socks. "What are we having?"

"Pizza. What kind do you want?" Bailey was already dialing the number of Minsky's Pizza. It's the one phone number we all know by heart.

"The usual," I said. I could already taste the gooey cheese and spicy tomato sauce.

"I'd like one small pepperoni and mushroom pizza," Bailey said into the phone.

I tugged on his shirt. "Don't you want to get a large?" I asked.

Bailey shook his head. "Hold on," he said to the person on the phone. "I'm not eating, Claud. I'm going to leave money for you to pay."

Bailey gave Minsky's our address and hung up. "You're not going to eat with me?" I asked.

"Can't," Bailey said. "I need to get to the library. I've got a huge history paper due on Monday. And with all this tax stuff going on, I haven't even started doing my research."

I perched on a wooden kitchen stool. "How did your meeting with Mr. Lemon Face go?"

Bailey picked up his jacket. "Could have been better. Could have been worse."

I swung my feet back and forth. I wasn't even sure I wanted to ask my next question. "Do you think the IRS might really decide to call social services?"

Bailey zipped up his jacket. He walked over to my stool. "I think we're going to be okay," he said in a serious voice. He reached over and messed up my hair. That's one of his favorite "big brother" gestures.

"Really?" I asked.

He grinned. "Really. I promise."

I breathed a big sigh of relief. If Bailey made a promise, I knew I could count on him. Now all I had to worry about was the competition. "Someone has to give me a ride to Berkeley tomorrow," I reminded him. "I've got to be there by two o'clock."

Bailey nodded. "No problem."

I sat up a little straighter. "Hey, do you want to hear my piece before you go to the library?"

Bailey plucked the car keys off the counter. "I'd love to, Claud. But I've really got to get going."

"I guess you'll just have to hear it at the competition tomorrow," I called. Bailey was already halfway out of the kitchen.

"We'll see," he said.

Then he was gone. I propped my elbows on the kitchen counter and frowned. *We'll see?* What was that supposed to mean?

Wasn't Bailey coming to my competition? I mean, this was a big one. An important one. He wouldn't miss it.

Would he?

# chapter seven

When I opened my eyes Saturday morning, the house was still dark. And except for a couple of birds singing outside, I was surrounded by complete silence.

I glanced at my digital clock—5:59 A.M. Wow! I considered any time before six o'clock the middle of the night. But there was no way I'd be able to fall back asleep. My stomach was full of butterflies—big butterflies with huge wings.

Today was the Northern California Junior Music Championship. The biggest competition of my life. I was already so wide awake, I felt as if I'd been up for hours.

I slid out of my sleeping bag. The morning air was cool, but luckily I was wearing my favorite green plaid flannel pajamas. I grabbed the red wool socks I'd been wearing last night and pulled them onto my feet.

I unzipped the flap of my tent and crawled into the dining room. The clock on the wall said it was now five minutes past six o'clock. Officially morning.

I could fix breakfast—I had time to make anything I wanted. A vision of bacon, pancakes, and scrambled eggs floated in front of my eyes. But as soon as I imagined myself taking a bite of food, my stomach let my brain know that eating was *not* a good idea. Butterflies and pancakes don't mix.

I drifted toward the stairs. Maybe I could practice my piece for Bailey. Last night he said he would love to hear it. And I could fix breakfast for him even if I didn't want to eat anything myself.

I tiptoed up the first flight of stairs. I didn't want to wake up Owen. Then I climbed the second flight of stairs. Bailey's room used to be our attic.

I tapped on the door. From inside I could hear Bailey snoring. "Bay?" I called. No answer.

I opened the door and peeked into the room. Bailey was sprawled across the top of his bed. He was wearing a pair of pajamas that were almost identical to mine. "Bay!" I said a little louder.

He mumbled something I couldn't understand. Then he turned over. Waking up Bailey was obviously going to be harder than I had thought. I crossed the room and stood over the bed.

I leaned over and shook his shoulder as hard as I could. "Bailey!" I shouted in his ear.

His eyes opened halfway. "Claudia?"

"Good morning!" I said cheerfully.

Bailey opened his eyes wider. "Is something wrong with Owen?"

I shook my head. "No. I was just wondering if you want to hear my Mozart now."

"Go away." Bailey pulled his pillow over his face. "It's too early."

"Well, how about some breakfast? I could play the piece after you eat."

"Later, Claud."

"Are you sure?" I asked. "Listening to music is a great way to wake up."

He moved the pillow and scowled at me. "Claud, I'm sleeping." He pulled his blanket over his head.

"Fine, fine," I said, backing toward the door. "I just thought I'd ask."

But Bailey wasn't listening. From underneath the blanket came a loud, long snore.

"I guess I'll go practice in the basement again," I muttered. "After all, I wouldn't want to disturb anyone's precious sleep."

\*   \*   \*

"Oh, no!" I cried out several hours later.

I fell asleep—in the basement! I pushed myself off the beanbag chair I'd been napping in and rubbed my eyes. Could it really be one o'clock in the afternoon? Maybe my watch had stopped—or suddenly sped forward.

I charged up the basement stairs, trying to figure out just what had happened. After I left Bailey's room, I had gotten dressed in the dumb red skirt that I absolutely did *not* want to wear. Then I went down to the basement to run through my piece a few times.

But somewhere during the third time playing my piece, I started to feel a little sleepy. After all, I hadn't slept much last night. So I decided to rest on the beanbag for a few minutes. And then my eyes had sort of closed. . . .

I burst through the basement door, ready to punch someone in the nose. *Someone* should have come down to wake me up. "BaileyCharlieJulia!" I screamed. "Owen!"

The house was totally silent. I glanced up at the kitchen clock. *It really was one o'clock!*

"Bailey!" I yelled again. He had to be here somewhere.

I raced through the kitchen and up the stairs. "Charlie! Julia!"

I opened Julia's door. Her room was empty. I crossed

the hall and opened Charlie's door. His room was empty. With a feeling of dread I sprinted down the hall. I opened Owen's door. Empty.

"Bailey!" I wailed, running up the steep attic stairs. "We need to go!" He couldn't still be asleep. Could he?

Bailey's door was wide open. "Let's go!" I shouted. My eyes darted around his room. Bailey wasn't there.

*This is not happening,* I told myself. I raced back down the stairs. *They did not forget about my competition.*

By the time I got downstairs, my heart was beating about a thousand times a second. I yanked open the front door and stared at the driveway. The car was gone.

There was no doubt about it. My family had abandoned me.

What was I going to do? I ran into the kitchen. Maybe I can find Charlie, I prayed. In record time I dialed the number of Salinger's.

"Salinger's. Good afternoon," Charlie said pleasantly.

"Charlie!" I screamed. "You've got to take me to the competition!"

On the other end of the line there was a long silence. "I thought Bailey was taking you."

"Well, I guess he thought *you* were taking me. And you all left the house without even *noticing* I wasn't around."

"Uh, sorry, Claud," Charlie stammered. I guess the panic in my voice got to him. "I'll be right there."

"Sure, unless you *forget*," I snapped.

As I hung up the phone, the doorbell rang. My heart leapt. Maybe it was Bailey. But why would Bailey ring the bell? Maybe it was Jody, and her mom could give me a ride so I wouldn't have to wait for Charlie.

The person at the door was not Bailey. Or Jody. "Hi, I'm Suzanne Teevan," the young woman standing on the porch greeted me. She was wearing a navy blue skirt and jacket. Her blond hair was up in a tight bun. She held out her hand.

"Uh, we're not interested in buying anything," I told her. "And I'm kind of in a hurry."

Suzanne Teevan laughed. I noticed she had a nice smile—really white teeth. She didn't look much like a door-to-door saleswoman. "I'm not selling anything," she explained. "I'm your tax auditor."

I gasped.

This was bad. Even worse than having no ride to the competition. How could everyone have forgotten that the auditor was coming today? This woman had the power to split up our entire family—and no one even bothered to show up to see her.

How could they have forgotten? *How?*

I opened the door wide and laughed nervously. "I was just joking," I said brightly. "I'm Claudia Salinger."

Ms. Teevan entered the front hall. She looked from side to side, as if she were studying every detail of our house. "Nice to meet you, Claudia. Is Charlie Salinger home?"

I laughed again. "Uh, why don't you come sit in the kitchen," I suggested. I needed to stall for time. "Charlie will be right home. He's *very* responsible."

"Good. I'm glad to hear it," Ms. Teevan answered.

"Charlie is just running a tiny bit late," I continued. "But he asked me to tell you how sorry he is to keep you waiting."

Ms. Teevan nodded. "The kitchen?" she reminded me.

"Right. The kitchen." I led her down the hall. "While we're waiting for Charlie, I'll tell you about all the responsible things he does around the house. . . ."

"Thanks for covering for me, Claud," Charlie said when we finally climbed into his pickup truck.

I slammed the door. "I can't believe you forgot she was coming." I was so mad, I could feel the veins in my forehead trying to pop out.

"I didn't *forget,*" Charlie insisted. "I thought she was coming at *three* o'clock."

I clicked my seat belt into place. "I guess it's just my major competition that slipped your mind, then."

75

Charlie peeled out of the driveway. "Claudia, I'm really and truly sorry that we all left this morning. We've all had a lot on our minds."

"Well, so have I," I snapped.

"Let's just get you to Berkeley as fast as we can. I need to get back to Suzanne Teevan before she snoops through the entire house."

I hugged my violin case close to my chest. "Fine with me."

Charlie braked for a red light. "She's really pretty, huh?"

"Who?" I was silently counting to ten, hoping the light would turn green before I finished.

"Suzanne. She doesn't look like a tax auditor."

The light turned green. "You are seriously messed up," I commented. Only Charlie could think about a woman's looks at a time like this.

I leaned back and closed my eyes. I was going to be late for the competition. Charlie wanted to date our tax auditor. And the rest of my family had left me to die in the basement. This day was not going the way I had planned.

"Can we just get there?" I yelled.

Charlie didn't say anything. Fine with me.

For the next twenty minutes we careened through the streets of San Francisco. Finally we crossed the

Bay Bridge, which led to Berkeley. I forced myself to relax.

If I was going to win the competition (if I even *got* there in time), then I had to push all my bad thoughts out of my brain. Music had to be my one and only focus.

"We're almost there," Charlie said. "You'll make it."

"Let's just hope *Suzanne* isn't getting impatient," I said. I wasn't ready to make up with Charlie. I was still furious.

He pulled up at the edge of Berkeley's enormous campus. "Last stop," he sang.

I stared at him.

"But I don't even know where I'm supposed to go!" I cried. "Aren't you going to come in with me?"

Charlie didn't even bother to put the truck in Park. "I can't. I have to get back to the audit."

I unbuckled my seat belt. Then I kicked open the door of the truck. "How am I supposed to find my building?" I demanded.

Charlie patted me on the shoulder. "Just ask someone. They can tell you where to go."

I jumped to the curb. "Thanks a lot." I shut the truck door with all the strength I had.

Charlie's face appeared at the passenger side window. "Good luck, Claud. You're going to be sensational."

Then Charlie—and the truck—sped down the road. I

stared at my feet for a moment. The sidewalk looked blurry through the tears in my eyes.

*You are not going to cry,* I told myself. *You don't have time. You can do this by yourself.*

With a sigh I turned toward the campus.

I still had no idea where I was supposed to go. I peered at my watch.

The competition was starting . . . now.

# chapter eight

"Excuse me," I called to a girl wearing bell-bottom jeans and a quilted vest.

"Yeah?" She turned and looked at me as if I were a bug under a microscope. I guess she wasn't used to seeing twelve-year-olds roaming the college campus.

"Can you tell me where Zellerbach Hall is?" I asked.

"Sorry. I'm into biology. I don't know where anyone does music." She continued down the path, her bell bottoms swinging in the wind.

"Great. Thanks for helping," I muttered.

"Hey, do you know where Zellerbach Hall is?" I called to another wandering student. This time I picked a guy about Charlie's age. He was wearing a suit and carrying a briefcase. On Saturday.

He stopped. "Zellerbach Hall? Let me think."

The guy looked like he was trying to do long division in his head. He stared into space and frowned with concentration. I tapped my foot impatiently.

"We're at the westernmost point of the campus now," he finally said. "If you turn yourself one hundred and eighty degrees, you'll be on a direct path to the quad at the center of campus. When you reach the quad, veer left at a forty-degree angle—"

"Can you just show me where it is?" I interrupted. I was desperate.

He glanced at his watch. "Well, I'm late for a meeting at the business school. . . ."

"Please?" I begged. "I'm late for the most important day of my life. Please?"

He smiled. "Okay. Follow me."

Finally! I trotted after him, holding my violin case with both hands. Why couldn't I have an older brother who was more like this guy? *Responsible.*

By the time we reached Zellerbach Hall, I was panting. I felt like I'd just run ten laps around the track at Walt Whitman. But I was here. At last!

I waved to Ken, the business-school guy. Then I pulled open the heavy door of the music hall. Directly in front of my eyes was a yellow poster board: NORTHERN CALIFORNIA JUNIOR MUSIC CHAMPIONSHIP. I read the big block letters. An arrow pointed down the hall.

I sprinted forward. Finally I reached a door marked BACKSTAGE. For a few moments I stood in front of the door, trying to catch my breath.

Backstage, there was a large crowd of musicians. I felt nervous as I looked around. I'd never seen so many violins in one place. I made my way toward a woman holding a clipboard.

Just as I reached her, I heard a loud voice booming from the auditorium. "Claudia Salinger. Last call for Miss Claudia Salinger."

My heart jumped. I raced the final steps to the woman with the clipboard. "That's me!" I told her. "They just called me! I'm Claudia Salinger."

"Go, go!" she ordered. She pointed to a small space at the side of the stage curtain. "Through there. You're next!"

Next! I couldn't be next! I hadn't even had time to take my violin out of the case!

I walked onto the stage, forcing myself to take deep breaths. Inhale, exhale. Inhale, exhale.

A bright light lit the stage, so I couldn't see the audience clearly. But I could tell that the large auditorium was packed. And I was sure that Ross was out there somewhere, watching me.

I stopped in front of a small table at center stage. A vase of red roses stood on the table. I set down my violin case beside the vase.

*Relax, Claudia,* I told myself. *Remember what Ross taught you.* Ross had showed me how to relax before a big performance. He said anxiety could ruin even a great violinist's playing.

I lifted my violin from the case. *Breathe in . . . one, two, three. Breathe out . . . one, two, three.*

I set the photograph of Mom where I would be able to see it as I played. I stepped a few paces to the side of the table. I lifted my violin to my shoulder. "I'll be performing Mozart's Violin Sonata in G," I called to the invisible audience. I raised my bow.

*Ready, set, go.* The bow touched the strings of my violin.

The first note was perfect. And so was the second. I closed my eyes. The music poured from my violin. I smiled. I pretended I was performing at Carnegie Hall. This was my dream.

"All right, everybody," Mrs. Leota announced. That was the name of the woman with the clipboard. "Dinner break."

I pushed myself off the floor. After my performance I had headed backstage and listened to the other competitors. Almost everyone had been good. But none of their pieces had been as difficult to perform as mine. And I knew the judges gave higher scores for more challenging pieces.

I stood up. Not one, but *both* my legs had fallen asleep. I jumped up and down—first on my left foot, then on my right foot—trying to get rid of that pins and needles feeling.

I wonder how Sabrina Monteclaire did? I thought. She must have performed before me. I bet *her* mother drove her here on time, and helped her find the auditorium, and came in to watch.

I bounced up and down a few more times, shaking the last of the pins and needles out of my legs. I was ready to eat now. I wasn't nervous anymore. And I needed to find Ross. We could talk about my performance over bacon cheeseburgers and French fries. And spending time with Ross would keep my mind off other things. Like the fact that my family had forgotten about me this morning.

I went up to Mrs. Leota. I cleared my throat. "Excuse me?"

She glanced up from the clipboard. "Yes, dear?"

"Can you tell me where to find Ross Werkman? I want to meet him for dinner."

Mrs. Leota flipped through several sheets of paper. I stood on tiptoe, peering over her shoulder. She had about twenty pages full of schedules.

"I'm sorry," she said. "Ross Werkman is in the middle of judging the duets. He can't be disturbed."

I frowned. Ross hadn't been watching me perform after all. No one had.

I felt tears rush to my eyes. Then a soft hand gripped my shoulder. I spun around.

And found myself face-to-face with Sabrina Monteclaire's mother. "Hello, Claudia," she greeted me. Her voice was friendly.

"Hi." Behind her I saw Sabrina. She was surrounded by a crowd of people.

"Where's your family?" Mrs. Monteclaire inquired.

"Oh, uh, they couldn't come," I stammered, trying to hide my tears.

She clucked her tongue. "How sad."

I shrugged. "They're very busy people." *Busy going on dates and trying to pick up the IRS agent,* I added silently.

"Well, you absolutely must have dinner with us." She gestured to all the people standing around Sabrina.

I looked at the group again. From what I could tell, two sets of grandparents and a handful of various aunts and uncles had come to watch Sabrina perform.

I wasn't sure what to say. Eating dinner with Sabrina's family would be a lot more fun than eating alone. But I didn't want Mrs. Monteclaire to feel sorry for me.

I felt a burst of anger toward my brothers and sister.

If they were here, I wouldn't need strangers to feed me.

Mrs. Monteclaire was studying my face. "I insist," she declared.

"Thanks," I said as cheerfully as I could. "I'd love to."

At least I would have dinner with a family. Just not *my* family.

# chapter nine

H ow's the food, Claudia?" Mr. Monteclaire asked.

"Oh, great. Wonderful." I glanced down at my plate. Actually, my food was totally gross. Mrs. Monteclaire told me to order whatever I wanted. So I decided to try duck à l'orange. It tasted like a hockey puck.

We were at Pierre's Bistro, a small French restaurant at the edge of the Berkeley campus. I sat mushed between Sabrina's grandpa Fred and nana Mary. Grandpa Fred took a handkerchief out of his pocket and blew his nose about once every two minutes.

Mr. Monteclaire turned his attention back to Sabrina. "Now, sweetie, you weren't trying your best out on-stage today."

"Yes, I was," Sabrina insisted.

"Sabrina, don't be ridiculous," Mrs. Monteclaire exclaimed. "You couldn't have been doing your best. You missed notes that you hit right on target at practice the other day."

Sabrina looked miserable. "I was nervous," she said quietly.

"You need to polish those rough spots," Mr. Monteclaire continued. "You want to make it into the finals, don't you?"

Sabrina slumped in her chair. "I'll try to do better on the next round, Daddy. I promise."

All of a sudden I felt like gagging on my bread. Didn't these people realize that Sabrina had enough pressure as it was? Competing in front of hundreds of people—not to mention several judges—would give anyone major butterflies. What kind of family couldn't understand that?

"I don't think Sabrina practices enough," Aunt Sophie stated. She sat across the table from me, next to Uncle Bernard.

Mrs. Monteclaire nodded as if her sister (at least I *think* Aunt Sophie was her sister) had just revealed the mystery of the universe.

Sabrina glanced over at me. She was squeezed between her grandpa Lionel and grandma Violet. Her face turned bright red.

At first I had been jealous of Sabrina because her whole family came to watch her compete. But now I felt sorry for her. I mean, I wanted my family to care about my music. But Sabrina's family cared *too* much!

I pushed back my chair and stood up.

"Why don't we go ahead and walk back to the music hall," I suggested to Sabrina. "We can get in some last-minute practice before the second round of competition starts."

Mrs. Monteclaire's face brightened. "Why, Claudia, what a wonderful idea!"

"Sounds good to me," Sabrina said.

Flashing a fake smile, I thanked Sabrina's parents for dinner. Then I waited while Sabrina walked around the table, kissing each of her relatives on the cheek.

"Good luck!" everyone called as we walked toward the door.

And then we were outside. I smiled at Sabrina. We had escaped!

"You sound good," I said to Sabrina half an hour later. She had completed a run-through of her Brahms piece.

From the restaurant we had gone straight back to Zellerbach Hall. I guess all her parents' complaining had made Sabrina eager to "polish the rough spots."

She *did* sound good. Actually, she sounded great.

"Thanks." She set her violin back in its case. "I just hope I make it into the finals. My dad will be so mad if I don't."

Sabrina sat down on the floor and leaned her back against the wall. She looked tired. I dropped down next to her and stretched my legs out in front of me.

"You will," I said.

Sabrina held out her hands. They were shaking. "I don't know. I get so scared onstage," she murmured.

"Didn't Ross teach you his relaxation techniques?" I asked.

Sabrina frowned. "I think so. But I forgot them."

"Watch me," I instructed Sabrina. I crossed my legs Indian-style. I placed one hand—palm up—on each of my knees. Then I formed two circles with my thumbs and index fingers.

"What are you *doing?*" Sabrina giggled.

I grinned. "This is a yoga position. Yoga is some ancient form of exercise. It's supposed to, like, join your mind and body so you can concentrate better."

Sabrina shrugged. "Whatever works." She copied my pose.

"Now slowly breathe in and out," I said. "And close your eyes."

"I'm still nervous," Sabrina commented.

"Inhale, exhale," I said. "Just give this a chance. After a few more breaths, I promise you'll feel better."

I counted silently to thirty. "Okay, now picture yourself at a very peaceful place," I continued. I tried to sound like Ross did when he taught me.

"Like where?" Sabrina asked.

"Anywhere. A lake, or maybe the top of a mountain."

"Got it," Sabrina said after a few seconds. "Now what?"

"You feel very calm," I said. "You're relaxed and confident. Your world is in complete harmony."

I breathed in and out a few more times. "Your mind and body are totally connected," I went on. "The music will flow easily from your violin. . . ."

After a few more moments Sabrina opened her eyes. "Wow! This stuff really works."

I smiled. "Great. Now maybe you can really *enjoy* performing."

Sabrina crossed her arms in front of her chest. "I don't know if I'll actually be able to enjoy it. I mean, this competition is a big deal. It could make or break my career."

Her *career?* I thought we were a little young to be caring about our careers. I was still worried about the senior prom.

"Do you want to be a professional violinist some-day?" I asked.

Sabrina shrugged. "I guess so. I mean, my parents talk about it all the time."

I thought of my own mother. She had loved the violin. But I couldn't imagine her pushing me to make the instrument my career. She would have said the decision was up to me.

"It must be hard to have your family breathing down your neck about the violin all the time," I commented.

"What do you mean?" Sabrina asked.

"You know. The way they were discussing every note you played while we ate dinner. It was like you weren't even in the room."

She shrugged. "I'm used to it."

"Wow! I don't think I'd be able to stand it. Your parents are seriously intense."

Sabrina gave me a cold stare. Oops. I guess I said the wrong thing. "At least *they* care," she sniffed.

"What's that supposed to mean?" I demanded.

"What kind of parents do you have anyway? They didn't even bother to show up for your big competition."

"My parents died," I said.

I've never found an easy way to tell people that I'm an orphan. Each time I tell someone that Mom and Dad are dead, I feel like it's the first time I'm saying the words. But I try not to get upset.

I watched as the color drained from Sabrina's face. "Oh. I'm, uh, really sorry," she stammered.

"That's okay," I told her.

Sabrina stood up. "I better, uh, go find my family," she stuttered. "They probably want to kiss me for luck."

"Whatever," I responded. A moment later Sabrina was gone.

"Sabrina Monteclaire," the voice from the auditorium boomed.

I was sitting backstage listening to the second round of performances. I hadn't seen Sabrina since she went to look for her family an hour before. But I'd been thinking about our talk nonstop.

I glanced toward the stage, trying to catch sight of Sabrina. She was clutching her violin tightly. She looked as if she were going to throw up.

"Good luck," I called.

Sabrina glanced at me. "Uh, thanks," she said, moving her gaze to somewhere behind my feet. Sabrina continued toward the stage without another word. I sighed. Moments later I listened as Sabrina started her piece.

I tried to concentrate on her performance. But instead my mind drifted back to what she had said about my family. What kind of family *did* I have? Why *weren't* they here? Wasn't it bad enough that I didn't have parents? I deserved attention from the family I had left. But no. They were all too busy to do something boring like coming to the biggest competition of my life.

I still felt sorry for Sabrina. I mean, her parents were total nightmares. But at least they were here. They cared. I would have given anything to have my mom and dad nagging me about practicing the violin.

Nagging me about *anything*.

I opened my violin case and took out the photograph of my mom. "I miss you," I whispered.

I listened to the last notes of Sabrina's piece. She had played well. Probably well enough to get to the finals tomorrow. And her whole family would be here to cheer her on.

But nobody would be here for me. Nobody in my family cared about me at all. I should have gone to the mixer tonight, I thought. I bet Charlie, Julia, and Bailey would never even have noticed that I skipped a violin competition.

I glanced at my watch. It was already eight o'clock. Jody was on her way to the mixer at this very moment.

She, Caroline, and Tiffany were going together. *I wish Jody could have come to watch me this afternoon,* I thought. *At least I would have had* someone *here with me.*

Mrs. Leota approached with her clipboard. "You're next, Claudia," she told me. "Good luck."

"Oh. Thanks." I pushed myself off the floor and walked slowly toward the stage entrance.

I tried to repeat the relaxation exercises I'd done earlier. But suddenly I couldn't remember anything Ross had taught me. How could I relax when I was all alone at the biggest competition of my life?

"Claudia Salinger," the announcer called.

I stepped on the stage. *Focus, Claudia,* I ordered myself. For the second time that day I placed my violin case and the picture of Mom on the small table at center stage. *Focus.*

I raised my violin. *My family should be here right now,* I thought as I lifted my bow. *If they loved me at all, they would never leave me alone this way.*

"Ms. Salinger, you may begin," the voice boomed.

I blinked. My thoughts had totally wandered! I hadn't even started my piece on time. Frantically I tried to remember the first few notes of Mozart's Violin Sonata in G.

"Please begin *now,*" the voice repeated.

I took a deep breath, and the notes of the music came rushing back to me. I began.

But my concentration was shot. And as I slid my bow across the strings of my violin, I knew this was going to be one of the worst performances of my life.

And I didn't even care.

# chapter ten

Great job, Claudia," Mrs. Leota said as I slouched offstage.

"*Please.* I stank." I wasn't going to pretend my performance had been anything but totally horrible.

*You don't care,* I told myself. *You don't care that you just messed up the biggest competition of your life. Nobody else cares, so why should you?*

But I *did* care. I felt like crying.

"Now, Claudia . . ." Mrs. Leota's voice had that really annoying tone that adults use when they're afraid that a kid is going to throw a temper tantrum.

"Can you just tell me where the duets competition is being held?" I asked.

She consulted the clipboard. "Hertz Hall."

"Thanks."

I spun on my heel and strode toward the door. I couldn't get to Hertz Hall—wherever it was—fast enough. I had to see Ross.

Outside, the night was cool and dark. Like an idiot, I had left my jean jacket at home. Of course, if I hadn't had to rush around like a maniac in order to get to Berkeley on time, I would have remembered to bring it. *Thanks, Charlie.*

I had no idea how to get where I was going—again. "Can you tell me where Hertz Hall is?" I called to a young woman holding a flute case.

She nodded. "See that path?" She pointed across the large lawn in front of Zellerbach Hall.

"Yep."

"Follow that path all the way across campus," she instructed. "You can't miss it."

"How far is it?" I asked.

She shrugged. "It's a quite a way." She seemed to notice the miserable look on my face. "Don't worry. The path is well lit. And there are hundreds of people around for the music competition."

I guess she thought I was scared about walking alone at night. I wasn't. I was just upset. And the last thing I felt like doing was hiking half a mile in my uncomfortable dress shoes. But I didn't have a choice.

"Thanks," I said. I took off down the path.

I felt about ten blisters forming on my feet. My family didn't remember that I was alive. And I probably wouldn't even make it into the finals tomorrow. But I knew Ross would make me feel better. He always did. For a long time after my parents died, he'd been the only person who could make me laugh.

At last Hertz Hall loomed at the end of the path. There were bright lights out front, and lots of people on the building's front steps. I went up to a guy who was tuning his violin.

"Do you know Ross Werkman?" I asked.

"Is he really tall?" the guy asked. "With black curly hair?"

I shook my head. "Thanks anyway," I answered. Ross most definitely did not have black hair.

I started to move to the next musician.

"Claudia?"

I turned around. Ross was jogging toward me.

"I'm so glad I found you," I exclaimed. I'd never been so happy to see anybody in my life.

"Is something wrong? What are you doing here?" Ross had a look of panic on his face.

"No, I'm fine. Well, sort of. I guess it depends on your definition of 'fine.'"

Ross seemed to relax. "Well, why aren't you at your competition?"

"I'm done."

Ross studied my face for a moment. "You don't look happy."

"I was terrible," I moaned.

Ross patted my shoulder. "Come on, Claud. I'm sure it wasn't that bad. Your first-round performance was amazing."

"You saw me?" I cried. "You were there?"

Ross frowned. "Well, not really," he admitted. "But I sent someone in to see how you did, and they said you were amazing."

"Oh," I replied. "Well, my second round stank."

He sighed. "So? What happened? What went wrong?"

"Can we sit down?" I pleaded. "My feet are killing me." I held up my left foot so he could see what uncomfortable shoes I was wearing.

Ross glanced over his shoulder. He waved at a group of people standing near the door. "Okay. But only for a minute."

I collapsed onto one of the stone steps. "You won't *believe* the day I had," I told him.

He sat down next to me. "Tell me about it—quickly."

"Well, I woke up at, like, five o'clock in the morning." I paused. "Okay, maybe not *five,* but it was early. And I was too nervous to eat breakfast, so I decided to wake up Bailey. See, I'd promised to play him the Mozart. Only Bailey was really tired, and he absolutely *refused* to get out of bed—"

"Claudia," Ross interrupted me. He looked impatient.

"Yeah?"

"You're going to have to speed up the story a little. I've got to get back to the judges' table as soon as possible. We have a lot of decisions to make."

I raised my eyebrows the way Julia does whenever one of her boyfriends says something annoying. *"Excuse* me," I said icily. "I thought I was talking to someone who cared."

Ross ran his fingers through his hair, which made his bangs stick up straight in the air. "Of course I care. But I'm pressed for time."

I nodded. "First of all, nobody in my family remembered I needed a ride to the competition. And forget coming to watch! They couldn't be bothered."

Ross looked sympathetic. I felt a little better.

"Secondly . . . is 'secondly' a word?"

"We'll say it's a word, Claud. Go on." Ross smiled, but I could tell he wasn't paying much attention to my story.

"Well, I was stuck eating dinner at a fancy restaurant with the Monteclaires. . . ."

"Uh-huh." Ross wasn't even looking at me. He was peering over my shoulder. A woman waved at him with one hand and pointed to her watch with the other.

"Ross? Are you listening?" I asked.

He turned back to me. "I'm sorry, Claudia. It sounds like you've had a rough day. But—"

"Ross!" the woman yelled. "We need to get back inside."

Ross gave me an apologetic smile. "I'm sorry, Claudia. I've got to get going."

"But—"

"Why don't you go back over to Zellerbach Hall. You can wait for the results of today's competition."

"I don't want—"

"I'll come find you after I'm done with the judging," Ross promised. "We'll talk then, Claud."

He gave me another pat on the shoulder and stood up. "I've got to go."

Without another word Ross was gone. I was alone. Again.

I stood at the exact spot where Charlie was supposed to pick me up at ten o'clock. But I wasn't waiting for Charlie. I had called myself a cab.

What did I care if Charlie drove up and I wasn't

where he expected me to be? He probably wouldn't even remember to come.

I thought about the finals tomorrow. If by some miracle I did make it into the last round of competition, I wasn't going to be there. Caroline Suh was right. Life was passing me by. The violin had been taking way too much of my time.

Let Sabrina win the Northern California Junior Music Championship. At least *her* family *cared* whether or not she was the best violin player in northern California.

I had spent the last week worrying about not letting anyone down. But now everyone I loved had let me down. Maybe I shouldn't even be stressing out over the tax audit. Did it really matter if the IRS split us up? I already felt as if I were alone in the world.

My family didn't care about my music. They didn't even care about me.

Finally, a yellow cab pulled up at the curb. I glanced at Berkeley's campus. Back there was my old life of violin practice, recitals, and competitions. This cab was going to take me to my new life—which would be filled with parties, dances, and the senior prom.

I hopped into the backseat of the cab. "Where you headed?" the driver asked.

I smiled at him in the rearview mirror. "I'm meeting my friends," I told him. "At the Walt Whitman Junior High mixer."

He pulled away from the curb. I leaned forward to tap him on the shoulder. "And step on it."

# chapter eleven

When the cab stopped in front of Walt Whitman Junior High, I was bouncing up and down on the seat with excitement. I couldn't wait to get inside and see my friends.

"Thanks for the ride, Max," I said to the driver. I handed him fifteen dollars—all the money I had. "Keep the change."

"You're welcome, Claudia. Have fun at the mixer." For the last fifteen minutes I'd poured out the whole story of my day to Max. He had turned out to be the friendliest cabdriver in history. He told me to put my bad day behind me and enjoy the rest of the evening.

I grinned. "I will."

I scooted out of the cab and jogged toward the side of the school, where there was a door that led straight into the gym. As I ran, my violin case bumped against my knee.

I opened the door of the gymnasium and stepped inside. During the school day the gym is filled with bright orange lights, the sound of sneakers squeaking against the hardwood floor, and the smell of sweaty socks. But tonight the place was totally different.

The lights were dim, and the decorations that Mrs. Wilensky's art class had started putting up the other day looked beautiful. But it still smelled like sweaty socks.

The gym was filled with boys wearing khaki pants, ties, and sport jackets. Most of the girls had on mini-dresses and high heels. Laughter echoed against the walls. Everyone seemed to be having a great time.

But something was missing. What? I stood still, gazing around the room. Wait a second. There was no music playing! How could a dance not have any music?

That's when I noticed that a lot of the kids were drifting toward me. Actually they were drifting toward the door behind me. Suddenly the lights brightened. I realized what was going on.

The mixer was over.

"Yo, Claudia!" Jeff Bloch walked toward me. His navy blue and red striped tie stuck out of the pocket of his jacket. His shirt had a big punch stain across the front.

"Hey, Jeff." I took a couple of steps away from the door so that a group of kids could pass by.

"You made it after all. Cool!"

I looked around the gym. The floor was covered with torn streamers and popped balloons. "I guess I'm late."

"So you weren't here to see Jody in the limbo contest?" Jeff asked.

"Uh, no."

Jeff laughed out loud. "It was hilarious. Mrs. Grant and Mr. Feldman were holding the pole. And Jody, like, didn't even—"

"Have you seen Jody?" I interrupted. I didn't want to be rude, but I absolutely had to find my best friend before she left the mixer.

"She's somewhere around here," Jeff answered. "I think I saw her near the punch bowl."

"Thanks, Jeff." I gave him a wave and took off across the gym.

"Catch you later!" Jeff called.

The mixer was over, but the gym was still packed. I pushed my way through a crowd of people. "Excuse me," I said, squeezing through the middle of two big guys who were trying to smash Coke cans against their foreheads.

As I walked, I scanned the gym. So far I didn't see Jody. Then I noticed a girl with red hair, wearing a black dress. Her back was to me. "Jody?" I called.

"Oomph," I cried a second later. I had been staring so hard at the redhead that I'd walked smack into a boy and girl. They had their arms wrapped around each other. Their lips were practically glued together.

"Hey, watch it!" the guy shouted. I recognized him right away. His name was Jack Starks, and he was on the eighth-grade football team.

"Oh, uh . . . sorry," I stammered. Meanwhile the redheaded girl turned around. She wasn't Jody.

"We're trying to share a *private* moment," Jack's girlfriend, Brandi Martin, said angrily. Brandi is one of those super-annoying cheerleader types. She carries her pom-poms with her from class to class.

"Sorry!" I snapped. If they wanted to make out, why didn't they go into the corner or something?

I continued across the gym. Finally I saw Alissa Moore. She rode the school bus with Jody and me, and we had always been friendly to each other. Maybe she knew where Jody was.

Alissa was talking to Brad Metzger. They were an official couple. I should know—Alissa talked about Brad nonstop every day on the way to school.

"Hey, Alissa!" I called.

She turned away from Brad. "Oh, hi, Claudia," she called back. Then she faced Brad again.

"I *said* I was sorry," Brad shouted.

"I don't care," Alissa responded. "You've been acting like a total pig all night. Oink, oink."

"Uh, do you know where Jody is?" I interrupted.

"Huh?" Alissa looked at me again.

"Jody. Have you seen her?" I felt my face start to turn red. Neither Brad nor Alissa looked like they wanted to talk to me.

"No," Alissa said shortly. She turned back to Brad. "Anyway, I told you I didn't want to come here with Jason and Bernard. They're both jerks . . ." she continued.

"Nice talking to you too," I commented. But Alissa wasn't listening.

A second later I spotted Jody. She was standing next to the punch bowl. She wore the black minidress she'd told me about, and her hair looked like she'd actually let her mom do it with a curling iron. I'd never seen her look so much like a girl.

"Jody!" I shouted, trotting toward her.

"Claudia! You're here!" Jody held up her hand, and I gave her a high-five. "Yo, everybody," Jody called to Caroline, Teri, and Tiffany. "Salinger is here, complete with violin."

The others were standing a few feet away, laughing. Suddenly everyone turned and stared at me. Next to all of those short black dresses, I felt totally out of place in my stupid red skirt and white blouse. "Hey, guys," I called.

Then I grabbed Jody's arm. "I need to talk to you," I whispered.

Jody walked farther away from the group so no one would be able to hear our conversation. "So, how was tonight?" I asked.

She shrugged. "Dancing, punch, cute guys."

"So was it fun?" I asked. I was half hoping she would tell me the dance was boring. At least then I wouldn't feel like I'd missed out on so much.

"Are you kidding? I had a blast." Jody spun in a circle. "So, what do you think of my outfit? Cool, huh? It's from, like, the seventies."

"Way cool," I agreed. Once again I felt like a complete geek in my little-girl skirt and blouse.

"So listen, Pete Hennesey asked where you were tonight," Jody told me.

My heart leapt. For a second I forgot all about my horrible day. "He did?"

"Yep. He thought you would have been able to win the limbo contest, since you're, like, the shortest girl in the class."

"Oh." Well, at least he noticed I wasn't there. That was better than nothing.

Jody dropped onto the floor of the gym and pulled off

the black high-heeled shoes she was wearing. "So, what's up? Did you win our hundred bucks, or what?"

"Hardly." I sat down next to her. Then I leaned back, propping myself up with my elbows.

"Don't tell me you lost!" Jody exclaimed. "You should have been able to blow the rest of those losers out of the water."

"Maybe," I said. "But my days of playing the violin are history."

Jody sat up straighter and narrowed her eyes at me. "What do you mean?"

"I think I'm going to quit violin." The words felt strange coming out of my mouth. Now that I had actually said out loud that I was quitting, I felt sort of hollow inside. But I was sure the feeling would pass. I just needed to get used to my new life as a normal, nonmusical eighth-grader.

"Why do you want to do a dumb thing like that?" Jody demanded.

"I'm sick of missing out on stuff," I explained. "And since nobody in my family cares whether or not I play, what's the point?"

"Hold up," Jody said. "What do you mean, they don't care?"

"None of them came to the competition today. Charlie and Bailey didn't even remember that I needed a *ride.*" I kicked my violin case, which was sitting next to my foot. "Who needs it?"

Jody crossed her arms in front of her chest. "Claudia, you're not the fiddle girl because Charlie and Bailey and Julia want you to be. You're the fiddle girl because you've got major talent. Not to mention a hundred dollars in cash in your near future."

I sighed. Jody was trying to help. But she didn't understand how I felt. No one did. I mean, if I couldn't have parents the way everyone else did, at least I could do other things that normal girls got to do. Like go to dances, and go shopping.

Suddenly Jeff appeared at my side. "Do you want a ride home, Claud?" he asked. "My dad's waiting outside."

"Go ahead," Jody told me. "We've already got a full car anyway. Mrs. Suh promised to pick us up in her Mercedes convertible, and it's got, like, *no* room."

I held out my hand to Jeff. He grabbed my fingers and pulled me off the floor. "Let's get out of here," I told him.

"See you, Fiddle Girl," Jody called.

I turned around. "From now on you can just call me Claudia," I said.

As I opened the door of our house, my eyes were drooping. Today had been the longest day of my entire life. All I wanted to do was crawl into my sleeping bag. I planned to sleep until noon tomorrow.

I tiptoed into the dining room. I wanted to get into bed before anyone had a chance to see me—I was still mad at the whole family.

Charlie sat in a chair right in front of the flap of my tent.

"Claudia, where in the world have you been?" Charlie demanded. "Do you know how worried we were? Ross called from the competition. He said you disappeared. I got over there as fast as I could. But were you waiting for me? No. You were not."

Charlie paused long enough to take a deep breath. "Ross and I covered every inch of that campus," he continued. "Finally some girl—Sabrina I think her name was—said she saw you getting into a cab. A cab! Why did you call a cab when you knew I was coming to get you?"

I guess Charlie ran out of steam for the moment, because he just stopped talking and stared at me. I tapped my foot against the floor and examined my fingernails. "Are you through?"

Charlie stood up and started pacing back and forth in front of my tent. "No, I'm not through, as a matter of fact," he said angrily. "I'm nowhere near through with you yet."

I sank into the chair. "I hope you don't mind if I sit

down for the rest of this lecture," I said calmly. "My feet are killing me."

Charlie glared at me. "Claudia, you are a part of this family. And being part of a family includes certain responsibilities. Such as being where you're supposed to be when you're supposed to be there."

"Kind of like you were here to give me a ride this afternoon," I commented. "Not!"

Charlie bit his lip. He seemed to be trying to think of some excuse. "We're not talking about me," he finally stated. "We're talking about *you*." He rubbed his forehead. "Where have you been anyway?"

I kicked off my shoes. "I was at school."

"School? What were you doing at school?" Charlie started pacing again.

*"If* you ever bothered to ask me about my life, you'd know that the eighth-grade class had a mixer tonight," I said.

"A mixer?" he asked.

"A dance, Charlie."

"You're telling me that you had Ross and me ready to call the police and report a *kidnapping* so that you could go to a dance?"

I raised my eyebrows. "How was I supposed to know you guys would be worried? No one was worried when I fell asleep in the *basement* for six hours."

Charlie ran his hand through his thick brown hair. "All right. You know what, Claud?"

"What?"

"We're going to talk about this tomorrow. Because right now you need to go to bed. Ross told me you've got to be at the competition by nine o'clock for the finals."

I felt a rush of happiness—I'd made it into the finals!

*It doesn't matter,* I told myself quickly. *I'm not going to the competition tomorrow.*

I stood up and gave Charlie a cold smile. "Actually, I can sleep as late as I want," I informed him.

"Oh? And why is that?"

"Because I'm not *going* to the finals. As of tonight, I quit the violin."

I turned around and stalked into my tent.

# chapter twelve

"Claudia?" Charlie called. "Claudia, get out here and talk to me."

"I can't hear you," I called back. "I'm asleep."

I expected Charlie to tell me again to come out of the tent. But he didn't. He didn't say anything at all. I heard his footsteps fading as he walked out of the dining room and into the hallway.

"I'm turning out the lights," Charlie called from the hallway. A moment later I was sitting in darkness.

That was fine with me. I wanted to be alone. And the dark night matched my mood perfectly. I unbuttoned my blouse and wiggled out of my red skirt. *I'm never wearing this ugly thing again,* I promised myself.

I dug around under my sleeping bag until I found

what I was searching for—a red flannel nightshirt I'd left there a couple of mornings ago. I pulled the night-shirt over my head. Then I balled up my competition outfit and stuck it in the corner of the tent.

Finally I poked my head out of the tent. There was no one in sight. I crawled out into the dining room and reached for my violin case. I pulled the case into the tent, then zipped the flap behind me.

Even in the dark it took me just seconds to snap open my violin case. I probably could have done it in my sleep. I lifted out my violin.

I lay down on top of my sleeping bag, cradling the violin with my arms. I ran my hands over the smooth wood, then plucked each of the strings with my fingers. This violin had been a part of my life for a long time— as long as I could remember.

Before my parents died, I'd had a different violin. But it hadn't been nearly as nice. I still had it somewhere— on a shelf in the basement probably. But I never played it anymore. I used only this instrument. The one that my mom had played like magic . . .

*"Claudia, are you ready?" Mom asked. She lifted her violin to her shoulder. She was almost nine months pregnant with Owen, and she looked beautiful.*

*"I don't know if I remember the whole thing," I said to her.*

*She gave me a big smile. "You'll be fine. Just watch me."*

*"Get on with it already," Bailey called from the sofa. "I've got to get to my game."*

*"Be patient, Bay," Dad told him. "Great music can't be rushed."*

*I nodded to my mom. "I'm ready." I lifted my violin to my shoulder.*

*Julia stood up from her spot on the couch. "Ladies and gentlemen, I present Claudia and Diana Salinger. They will be performing a duet composed by the one and only Diana Salinger. The piece is called 'Saturdays.'"*

*My mom and I lifted our bows. We'd been practicing the duet all day—just the two of us. Playing the violin with Mom was my absolute favorite thing to do on Saturdays.*

*"One, two, three," my mom whispered to me. We began . . .*

I blinked my eyes rapidly, trying to hold back the tears. Mom and I must have performed that duet a hundred times after that day. But since she died, I hadn't played "Saturdays" once. Performing half a duet is about the most depressing thing in the world.

Suddenly I realized there was music playing. Violin music. It was coming from outside my tent. "Saturdays," I realized with a pang of sadness. That must be why I was thinking of it.

But what was going on? Who was playing Mom's music?

I set my violin down beside me. "Hello?" I called, sitting up. I unzipped the flap of my tent and crawled out into the dining room.

Charlie sat slouched in a chair in the corner. "It's just me, Claud," he said quietly.

"What are you doing down here?" I asked. As my eyes adjusted to the dim light, I saw that Charlie was holding a portable tape player on his lap.

"I felt like listening to this tape of you and Mom," Charlie answered. "Remember when we made this?"

I nodded. "Yeah. It was just a week before Mom and Dad died. You were over for dinner. And afterward Dad insisted we play you the new and improved version of 'Saturdays.'"

Charlie laughed softly. "You know, all I could think about was how I had a date later that night. I didn't think I had time to listen to you and Mom." He shook his head. "I'd give anything to be able to watch you two play together again."

"Yeah." I knew how he felt.

I wished a thousand times a day that I could watch my mom or dad do something that had seemed totally boring when they were alive. Like washing the dishes. Or sweeping the front steps.

"Can we talk, Claudia?" Charlie asked. "Please?"

"Are you done yelling at me?" I asked.

"Yes. I promise."

I shrugged. "Okay. If it's that important to you." I sat cross-legged on the carpet at Charlie's feet.

"Why don't you want to play the violin anymore, Claud?" he asked.

"I'm tired of it. The violin takes up too much of my time." I wrapped my arms around myself to keep warm.

Charlie leaned forward in his chair, resting his elbows on his knees. "Would you feel that way if Mom were still alive?" he asked.

"I don't know. A lot of things would be different if Mom and Dad were alive. I mean, you wouldn't even be living here."

Charlie nodded. "That's true. But you know how much it meant to Mom that she passed on her musical talent to you. Do you really want to give that up?"

I squeezed my eyes shut for a moment. "See, Charlie, this is the whole problem. You and Bay and Julia want me to play the violin because it reminds you of Mom. It's a way for all of you to keep her close. But nobody cares about the violin and what it means to me. Nobody cares about me at all."

Even in the dark I could see that Charlie looked shocked. "Claud, how can you say that?"

I shrugged. "Because it's true."

"If I didn't care about you, why would I be so worried when I couldn't find you at the competition?" he asked.

"Don't you understand, Charlie?" I almost shouted.

"Mom and Dad would never have left the competition at all. They would have been right there, the whole day—to cheer me on, and take me to dinner, and help me relax so I could play well. They would have acted like it was *important*."

"Claudia . . ." Charlie began.

I held up my hand to let him know I wasn't finished talking. "That's why I went to the mixer tonight, Charlie. To be with my friends—who care about me."

"But we all love you," Charlie responded. "So much."

"Then why didn't you come see me today?" I asked.

Charlie rested his head in his hands. "I'm sorry, Claudia. We should have been there."

"Yes, you should have." Finally there was *something* we agreed on.

"Things have just been crazy around here lately. The tax audit had us all running around. . . ."

"Still, one of you could have come," I pointed out. My voice was starting to tremble.

"And the audit was over by the time I started my second performance," I continued.

He nodded. "You're absolutely right."

"I mean, you guys didn't even *remember* I had the competition today. You can't blame that on the tax audit," I continued.

"You're right," Charlie repeated. "Claud, listen to me. You're totally right."

"I am?" I was surprised. I'd been expecting more lame excuses.

"Yes," Charlie assured me. "And you must be really mad at Julia, Bailey, and me. But you shouldn't take it out on your violin. You're too good to give up playing over something like this."

"I don't know . . ." I didn't feel angry at Charlie anymore. I just felt tired.

Charlie slid out of his chair. He sat down next to me on the floor. Then he looked me straight in the eye. "Besides, Claudia, the violin isn't just my link to Mom. It's yours too."

I blinked in surprise. He was right. I couldn't even look at a violin without thinking of my mom.

"Just listen to this," Charlie continued. He held up the small tape player. "You and Mom were amazing together."

I smiled. "We were kind of, weren't we?"

"Do you want to know a secret?" Charlie asked me.

"Sure," I responded. "What is it?"

"When Mom and Dad were alive, I was jealous of you."

I couldn't believe it. What reason could Charlie possibly have to be jealous of me? "I don't understand," I said.

"You and Mom always had this amazing connection," he continued. "When you guys played the violin together, it was like you were the only two people in the world." For a couple of seconds Charlie was quiet. "I know Mom loved me. She loved all of us. But she and I never shared the kind of special bond that you and she did."

I wasn't sure what to say. I'd never thought about the violin that way. It never even occurred to me that my brothers and sister wished *they* could play the violin. I just figured they thought it was something I had to do. Like breathing, and brushing my teeth.

Charlie stood up. "I can't tell you what to do, Claudia," he said softly. "You've got to live your life the way you decide is best. But I hope you'll really think about it before you pack away your violin forever."

Charlie switched off the tape player. Then he rested his hand on my head. " 'Night, Claudia."

"Good night, Charlie."

As Charlie walked out of the dining room, I crawled back into my tent. I wasn't sure if Charlie and I had made up exactly. I was still mad that no one remembered I needed a ride that afternoon.

But he had given me a lot to think about. I scooted into my sleeping bag and reached for my violin. Resting on my chest, the instrument rose and fell as I breathed.

I closed my eyes, feeling truly peaceful for the first time in days. I knew what I had to do.

# chapter thirteen

The streets of San Francisco were nearly empty as Charlie and I drove toward Berkeley on Sunday morning. I rolled down the window of the truck and stuck my head out into the fresh morning air.

"What are you doing, Claud?" Charlie asked, glancing sideways at me.

I pulled my head back inside. "Just enjoying the morning," I told him. "This drive is a lot nicer now that we don't have to go eighty miles an hour."

"Come on, Claud. I wasn't doing eighty yesterday. My truck doesn't even go that fast."

"Well, we were so late that I was *wishing* you'd go faster," I responded. "It's almost the same thing."

"Let's just be grateful that we're on time today,"

Charlie said. He rolled down his own window and rested his elbow on the door.

"Yeah, thank heaven for small favors," I said, quoting one of Dad's favorite phrases.

Charlie laughed. "Thank heaven for small favors," he repeated.

I leaned back in my seat and thought over the morning's events. When I crawled out of my tent at seven-thirty, I figured I would have to beg someone to take me to the competition.

But when I walked into the kitchen, the whole family was already there, fixing breakfast. I almost fainted with shock.

"What's going on?" I asked.

"We've all got a lot of stuff to do today," Julia replied as she poured batter into the waffle iron.

"Yeah," Bailey added. He was cutting bananas for Owen's cereal. "We wanted to get an early start."

Charlie looked up from the newspaper. "What about you, Claudia?" he asked. "Do you have anything to do today?"

"I've got to be at the final round of competition by nine o'clock," I said simply. I didn't think I needed to explain that I changed my mind about quitting the violin.

Charlie glanced at the clock. "We'll leave in forty-five minutes," he said. "Make sure you're ready."

Julia plopped a waffle and a piece of bacon onto a plate. "Better eat fast," she said, handing me the plate. "We've got to hurry if we're going to dig up something decent for you to wear."

And so here I was. I was dressed in one of Julia's short black dresses (well, on me it was sort of a long dress) and heading toward the finals of the biggest competition of my life. I could almost smell the hundred-dollar bill I planned to win.

The Berkeley campus came into view. It looked a lot nicer than it had when I left the night before.

Charlie brought the car to a stop—on the road next to Zellerbach Hall this time. Then he leaned over and hugged me close. "You know, I'm really proud of you, Claudia."

"I know," I said. And I did. Charlie had proved to me last night that he really did care about my violin playing. And he cared about *me*.

I untangled myself from his bear hug and grabbed my violin case. "Wait and see if I win before you say that," I told him.

Charlie shook his head. "Winning doesn't matter. What matters is that you're going to get out there and give the best performance you can give."

I jumped from the truck. "Thanks, Charlie. That means a lot to me."

I shut the door of the truck. I felt one hundred percent better than I had when Charlie had dropped me off yesterday. I still wished my family wanted to come hear me play, but I wasn't angry. I was performing for myself, not for anyone else.

I watched as Charlie sped off down the street. Then I turned toward Zellerbach Hall. I had a big morning ahead of me.


*Inhale, exhale,* I chanted silently. My eyes were closed, and I was sitting in the yoga position I'd shown Sabrina yesterday. The competition started in fifteen minutes. I wanted to be completely relaxed.

"Hi, Claudia," I heard a voice say.

I opened my eyes. "Hi, Sabrina." I was surprised to see her. I didn't think she ever wanted to speak to me again—she had acted so weird after I told her about my parents. But I was glad she had made it into the finals.

"I'm sorry about yesterday," Sabrina said. "I just felt like such a jerk for saying that thing about your parents. . . ."

"Don't worry about it," I told her. "You had no way of knowing."

"Well, I really am sorry . . . about your parents, I mean. Losing them must have been tough."

I patted my violin case. "They're still with me," I said. "I just can't see them anymore."

Mrs. Leota rushed over, clipboard in hand. "The competition is starting, girls," she told us. "Since there are only a few performers today, I want you all to line up in order."

I stood up. "Good luck, Sabrina."

"You too, Claudia," she responded.

Mrs. Leota began herding us into the line of performers. "Remember—inhale, exhale, inhale, exhale," Sabrina whispered.

We both giggled.

By the time it was my turn, I didn't need to do my relaxation exercises. I was totally calm.

"Ms. Claudia Salinger," the familiar voice of the announcer called.

I held my head high as I walked onto the stage. I felt my mother's presence all around me. It was almost as if she were here with me, holding my hand.

I'd left my violin case backstage, but the photograph of Mom was tucked into my pocket. I reached down to touch the picture. Then I took my place at center stage.

"I'll be performing Mozart's Violin Sonata in G," I announced in a clear, confident voice.

*This one is for you, Mom,* I said silently. I knew deep in my heart that I was about to give a perfect performance. I rested my violin against my shoulder, lifted my bow, and started to play.

The music flowed through my body. As my bow glided across the strings of my violin, I closed my eyes.

Memories of my mother drifted through my mind. I saw her standing on the street corner in front of our house. She was waiting for me to get off the bus at the end of a school day. Then I saw her tucked into her bed, holding a dictionary and a crossword puzzle.

I remembered the night Owen was born. We all went to the hospital to wait. After twelve hours of labor, Dad called the rest of us into Mom's hospital room. She was laughing and crying all at the same time. In her arms Owen seemed like a perfect little doll. She looked up and saw me standing at the door. "Meet your big sister," she said to Owen.

Finally I remembered the last time we'd played "Saturdays" together. "You've got real talent," she said to me. "Someday you're going to be better at playing the violin than I am."

The last notes of the Mozart floated from the strings of my violin. The sound of music faded in the auditorium. I removed my violin from my shoulder.

I opened my eyes. The audience was clapping wildly. From the back of the auditorium I heard whistles and cheers. I took a deep bow, holding my violin in one hand and my bow in the other.

"Thank you," I whispered.

I didn't know if I was thanking my mother, or myself, or maybe even my violin. I just knew I was glad to be here, doing what I love to do.

I walked offstage. The crowd was still cheering.

"This is it," Sabrina said nervously.

We filed back onto the stage. The judges were ready to announce the winner. "The big moment," I replied.

"I hope you win," Sabrina said. "You were the best."

I smiled. "Thanks."

We lined up across the stage. Isaac Molari, the director of the competition, strode out from behind the curtain.

He stopped in front of a microphone. "Ladies and gentlemen, it is my pleasure to announce the winner of the violin part of the Northern California Junior Music Championship," he said.

The crowd cheered. I held my breath.

Mr. Molari cleared his throat. The audience quieted down. "I present to you the youngest violinist ever to win this competition," he exclaimed. "Ms. Claudia Salinger!"

Time seemed to stand still. I did it. I won! Silently I thanked Charlie for making me realize how much the violin really meant to me.

I felt Sabrina nudge me. I walked toward Mr. Molari.

"Congratulations, Claudia," Mr. Molari said. He shook my hand. "Take a bow."

I took my bow, listening to the thunderous clapping. As I stood back up, I gazed into the audience. Up until this moment I had been so focused on my music that I hadn't even noticed the faces out there.

My mouth dropped open. In the front row Ross was standing, clapping his hands high above his head.

And in the seats next to him I saw Charlie, Bailey, Julia, and even Owen. Bailey was holding a sign. GO, CLAUD! the sign read in big bold letters.

My grin grew even bigger—if that was possible. My family had been there the whole time, cheering me on. And I hadn't even known it!

I had been wrong to doubt my brothers and sister. They loved me—with or without my violin!

"Everyone raise your glasses," Charlie announced.

"A toast to Claudia!" Bailey added.

I raised my cherry Coke. "Thanks everyone," I said.

We were at Salinger's, celebrating my victory. Charlie had even had the chef bake a special cake shaped like a violin.

I gazed around the table, smiling at each of my brothers and my sister. It felt great to have my family back.

"You haven't heard the great news," Julia said. She

stuffed a forkful of German chocolate cake into her mouth.

"What?" I asked.

"We cleared everything up with the IRS," Charlie exclaimed.

"How? I mean when? Where?" I was so happy, I felt like I would burst. Our family wasn't going to be split up!

"Suzanne Teevan called this morning," Charlie explained. "When she finished going through our paperwork, she realized we owe only a few hundred dollars."

"The IRS knows that we just made an honest mistake," Julia added. "We're in the clear."

Bailey swallowed a bite of cake. "Best of all, Suzanne gave Charlie a great tip on a deduction we can take next year," he said. "I bet we'll get a refund!"

I didn't know exactly what a tax deduction was. Or a refund. And I didn't care. Our problems were over—at least for now!

"What do you say you and I head to the mall?" Julia asked. She pushed away her empty plate.

"What for?" I asked.

"Jody called this morning. She's having a bunch of eighth-graders over for pizza tonight." Julia grinned. "And she wants you to come."

"Jody's having a party? Tonight?" This was great. Finally I was going to have a social life.

"Yep. And you need a new outfit. You don't want to wear your old overalls, do you?"

I grinned. "Thanks, Jules."

She shrugged. "Hey, what are big sisters for?"

I took a bite of cake. Big sisters were good for a lot of things! And so were big brothers. I glanced at Owen. Little brothers were pretty great too.

Yup. Life wasn't so bad. I had my violin. I had my friends. And I had my family.

At this moment I wanted only one more thing. I held up my plate. "More cake, please!" I exclaimed.

Charlie reached over and squeezed my shoulder. "Anything you want, Ms. Famous Musician."

I smiled. "I already have everything I want," I said.